Gideon: March

Mystic Zodiac

Book 3

Brandy Walker

Gideon, Mystic Zodiac
Copyright © 2015 Brandy Walker
Cover by TEZ Graphics, Brandy Walker
Image: © Curaphtography | Dreamstime.com
Image: © Starblue | Dreamstime.com
Edited by Noel Varner

Trademarks:

Jetboil– Johnson Outdoors
Jeep – Fiat Chrysler US LLC

First Electronic Print, Mar 2015

QUOTE:

I like my life how it is. I can do what I want, when I want. What more does a man need? ~ Gideon

SERIES BLURB:

Welcome to the Mystic Zodiac Series.

High atop Mount Olympus, the ancient Gods and Goddesses still reside, hidden from mortal view.

They have always been there.

WILL always be there.

Watching…

Judging…

Meddling.

They dabble in the lives of humans and lesser immortals, known as Mystics.

For fun. Out of boredom. Simply because they can.

They thrive on watching people squirm under their thumbs. Laugh and celebrate each other while plotting to top what they did.

This is where our story begins…

GIDEON BLURB:

A bet between Eros, the God of love & desire, and Chloe (Chlotho), the Fate of birth, leads to a year filled with match-making and passion.

~~~~~

Gideon Deckard is finally getting a little time away from the Keystone Predator Pack to go wolf. All he has planned is a week of running wild through the Grand Canyon before the hiking season starts back up. Once it does, he'll go back to what he does best...being the Alpha he was born to be.

Ryder Sparks can barely contain her excitement. She's taking a week off from work at the family store, Sparks Sporting & Outdoors, and going on her dream vacation. A four day hiking trip on a lesser traveled trek through the Grand Canyon. The season has opened early and she was the first to get the coveted pass. She's looking forward to pushing herself on her first solo trip and discovering who she was really meant to be.

A run in with a massive grey wolf has Ryder stumbling and getting knocked out. When she wakes up, she's back in her tent and there's a hunky man there to help her get back on her feet. When she finds out he's a wolf-shifter instead of freaking out, she decides to go on the adventure of a lifetime with him. Now all she has to do is convince Gideon to give her a chance to be his one and only Luna.

~~~~~

NOTE: Mystic Zodiac is a 12 book series. It is NOT a serial. Each book ends in a happily ever after for the main couple. However, the prologue and epilogue of each story follows the Gods that kick off the series, Eros and Chlotho (aka Chloe). At the end of the series the bet between the two will come to a conclusion.

MYSTIC ZODIAC: GIDEON

PROLOGUE

Eros made sure to get to the Parthenon early, finding the perfect spot to keep an eye out for Chloe. He didn't want her to have the advantage of surprise over him. Not when he knew she had completed the last challenge in two weeks time. He expected her to gloat about that particular fact and possibly use it to her advantage.

He never doubted she could do it. She had been correct in her assumption that Parvati would fall in love with her fated mate with speed and ease.

It was the human that he hadn't counted on falling so quickly. The man was older, in his mid thirties, and well established in life. There had been many chances for him to find someone and fall in love, yet he hadn't. The man's mother even attempted to set him up, but to no avail.

All's well that ends well though. Two months were complete with 10 more to go. The next couple would be a bit more problematic just based on the timeline. He'd get into that as soon as Chloe showed up.

1

As casually as possible, Eros glanced around the huge open building. People milled about chatting and conducting business. Others lounged and enjoyed the mead, fresh fruits and meats being carried around by servers. He had yet to see Chloe's dark head enter the room. The regal air about her was forever causing people to move out of her way. It was that and the fact that she held their lives in the palm of her hand. One wrong word and the Fates would come together and reevaluate your life.

As if by magic Chloe appeared before him. The statuesque brunette glided across the floor, her dark blue filmy dress catching on the breeze she created with her movements, fluttering around her ankles. She was truly a vision to behold. His cock started to fill and he had to force the sensation away. Their clothing did little to hide how the body reacted. Letting her see she affected him to any degree would be suicide when it came to their game.

Eros eased back into the pillows he was on as he waited for her. The raised corner of the room he'd picked was brimming with blankets and cushions. A few strategically placed pieces and she would never know what was happening beneath the thin cloth wrapped around his waist.

"Eros," she stated, head tilted up slightly.

"Chloe," he drawled.

"I didn't know you knew this hour of the day existed. It won't be midday for another three hours."

Eros chuckled and swept his hand out in invitation. "Come join me."

Chloe eyed the pillows speculatively, hesitating longer than he appreciated. "Don't worry, my sweet, I have no intention of doing *anything* with you." His pride still smarted after their last meeting. *You are nothing but a hot piece of ass I want for a small amount of time.* Chloe's words had screamed through his head at the most inopportune times during the last month. He was determined she would pay for them. If that meant dinging her pride, then he would – for now. He wouldn't allow her to leave in anger though. They would need to work together to speed things along this time.

Her surprised gaze whipped to his face. He masked the hurt that beat through him, plastering on a smug grin. Her eyes narrowed and she snarled.

Chloe dropped down onto the cushions in one graceful move. She opened her mouth to speak.

He cut her off before she had the chance. "Congratulations on your latest accomplishment."

She blinked rapidly, stunned by his words; mouth opening and closing without a sound.

"But then you said it wouldn't be difficult to match a goddess of love and devotion and I agree. Parvati's match was one that needed to be done. Not truly a challenge."

"None of your so-called matches will be. As I told you before, your gift is a joke. These humans and Mystics fall too easily. A trained monkey can do it."

Eros laughed loudly. "I shall let Zeus know you think so. He's up for fun and games. But tell me, Chloe, how difficult is *your* job. You are one of three. You decide life and that is it. Your sisters have the harder tasks of figuring out how long someone should live and when they should die. You only plant the seed."

Chloe moved to get up, and he grabbed her by the wrist stopping her. Rubbing his thumb along her delicate skin, he felt her pulse pick up. "Ready to give up your spot so soon?" He nodded to the cluster of women behind them. He'd known they were there, waiting for the moment they could join him. His popularity preceded him, and all knew when he was in the Parthenon he was looking for company.

Tugging on her lightly, he shifted her closer. "It isn't so nice to have someone tell you your job means nothing."

3

She pursed her lips in a sexy little pout and nodded slightly. He knew she wouldn't take the words back. He didn't want her to. They were what got them where they were, and he wouldn't have it any other way. Sparring with her excited him in a way he never felt, not even with the most skilled courtesan at his feet.

"Let's move on." He released her wrist and saw a flash of disappointment in her eyes. He grinned and let out a contented breath. "You will have less time this month to match my couple."

"I think I've already proven I don't need the entire month," she said smugly.

He snorted. "It wouldn't matter in this case. Two weeks will go by before they even make first contact. They will need to fall in love quickly."

"That shouldn't be a problem. Your Mystics are proving just as susceptible as humans. They desire love and acceptance just the same. With it being March, and the month of the shifters, all I need to do is get them in the same room. I doubt you would put together two who are not true mates. One whiff of the other and my job will be done."

"Not so fast, Chloe. This shifter's mate is human, she won't react to him the same way a shifter would. Gideon will know on contact, but she will not. He will have to convince her not only to be his mate but to take on the changing as well. That may not be too difficult, but the goal of our monthly challenge is to get them to fall in love. Gideon likes his life exactly how it is and has no intention of changing, even for his mate. He doesn't believe in love."

"If she is his mate then love will surely happen."

"It may over time, but you must make it happen in the span of fourteen days. That's *if* they meet the first day she is out there."

Chloe worried her lush, deep red bottom lip. Eros fought the urge to lean forward and soothe it. To run his

4

tongue over the spot, tasting the sweetness he knew would be there. "What do you mean by that? Meet when she first gets out there. Is she heading to his woods to prowl around?"

Eros reached out and grabbed a lock of her caramel-colored hair, wrapping it around his finger. "She is heading for a solo trip into the Grand Canyon. Hiking and camping for four or five days. I would need to double check the research on her, however."

Chloe wrinkled her nose. "Why would she do that?"

"That's the kind of woman she is, and one of the reasons she is meant for Gideon."

"I don't see how I can help in the matching. Theirs sounds like one of pure luck."

"This is where the fun part of my job comes in. Since it is you making the match, you will have to travel to the earthly realm and mingle with the humans."

A fire of excitement lit her eyes. Sitting up straighter, Chloe moved closer to him. She was within kissing range. Two months ago he'd placed a quick, soft kiss on her lips in this very room. It had been a momentary lapse in judgment, for after it was over; he'd wanted to do it again and again. There had been no chance before now. He breathed in slowly, pulling in her soft scent. His cock responded, twitching beneath the cloth again. He could easily tumble her onto her back and take advantage of her surprise. He'd finally feel what it was like to have her body beneath his. It would also put an end to their game, and he was far from ready to give it up.

"Mingle with them," she said, awed as if she never thought to do it. She probably didn't. Her life would have never given her the opportunity to travel outside Olympus. She had no need to be with commoners and those lesser than herself.

"Yes, I know what I had planned to help them along. Would you like to figure something out on your own or

5

have me tell you the best way to go about it?"

Chloe tapped her finger to her lips. "It is already the first of the month. Do I have time to come up with a plan?"

"You do."

Chloe nodded sharply. "Since the couple will not meet until later this month, I will send a message in a week to let you know what I have decided." She rose and Eros felt his heart drop. He wouldn't be getting that kiss this time either. "Until then," she said and left.

The gaggle of woman waiting for Chloe to leave approached, all collectively holding their breath. Eros frowned and stood. "Not today."

He followed Chloe's path out of the Parthenon and took off for his home. He was not in the mood for simpering bobble heads. This made two straight months where he felt no desire for them at all. None of his usual playthings intrigued him the way his tall, gorgeous Fate did. This was going to be a problem.

CHAPTER ONE

March 9 ~ 8am

Ryder practically bounced out of her Jeep, as she pulled to a stop at the Backcountry Information Center. It was odd for them to ask someone to pick up their permit in person, but she didn't mind. For months she'd planned this trip, making sure she did everything by the book to get the highly sought-after paper. The hardest part was waiting for the exact minute she could fax in her application. The backpacking permit she wanted was one of the hardest permits to get in the national park system, and she was determined to get one.

Four, possibly five, days of hiking and camping in the Grand Canyon on a solo trip, going from Grandview Point to the South Kaibab Trail. It was the best present she'd ever given herself.

Not that her roommate would agree with that. Pansy thought she was crazy for wanting to spend time walking around a — as she put it — "super old bunch of rocks." Pansy wasn't an outdoors kind of girl, which was funny because she was a fox-shifter.

To Ryder it sounded like heaven. She'd grown up hiking and camping with her family. Her love of the outdoors inherently ingrained into her soul. Nothing would ever take its place.

A woman in a green ranger outfit appeared in front of the doors. She unlocked it and waved Ryder forward. Ryder made sure she got there precisely when they opened. Hopefully it wouldn't take long, and she would get back in time for her shift at the store. She counted herself lucky that her boss was forgiving. It also didn't hurt that he was her dad. He knew her plans for the trip, and she'd called to let him know she had to pick up her permit.

The rangers probably wanted to make sure she could handle the solo trip. A lot of people mistook her for being younger than her twenty-four years. She attributed it to her healthy lifestyle and lack of sitting behind a desk.

She breezed into the building, making a beeline for the brunette ranger from before. A golden-haired man stood near her, and there was a strange undercurrent between them. Like a sexual tension neither wanted to acknowledge.

Not my problem. She shrugged and approached the desk. "Hi, I'm Ryder Sparks. I got a call about picking up my backcountry permit. I was told I had to get it today."

The female ranger looked at her and smiled. "Sure thing, hon." The southern twang that came out of her mouth threw Ryder off. She didn't looked like a Southerner. There was something almost ethereal about her. The blond fellow snickered, and the woman shot a glare his way.

"Okay," Ryder said under breath, dragging the word out. There was definitely something going on between the pair. When the woman just stood there glaring at the man, Ryder decided to move things along. "So, the permit?"

"Oh." The woman turned and blindly grabbed some paperwork. She slid it across the countertop, and Ryder

8

was surprised to see it was actually hers. "If I can get you to sign here and here," she pointed to two places without looking down, "I'll get you on your way."

"Thanks." Ryder snatched up the pen and was about to sign; she stopped and looked up at the woman. "Don't you need to see my ID or anything? Make sure I'm the person this paper says I am."

"Now, honey, why would anyone come in claiming to be someone they aren't for a four-day backcountry permit?" The southern drawl dripped from her lips, grating against Ryder's ears. "Besides darlin', you look like that picture you faxed in."

Ryder's brows furrowed. The woman hadn't even looked at the paperwork...but whatever. "Okay then." She signed quickly and pushed the paper back across the counter. The woman handed it to the man and picked up another slip of paper. She rubbed her fingers over it and cocked her head to the side. She nibbled on her lip, then cast a glance at the man, who drew up closer. "This is the right one, isn't it Cup...uh, Cupert?"

Cupert (and what a shitty name that must have been growing up) snatched the paper from her hand. He ran his fingers over it just like she did, then handed it to Ryder. "Looks to be. Here ya' go."

"Uh, thanks." Reaching out, she took it from the frowning man. The second her fingers touched it she felt a spark. Goosebumps rose on her flesh, and a shiver tripped down her spine.

"Make sure you don't lose it, and remember to clip it to your tent when camping." The man pushed over some brochures, which Ryder grabbed.

"Was there anything else?" Ryder looked between the rangers, fully expecting a lecture or something. There had to be a reason they wanted her to drive all the way from Flagstaff to pick the permit up.

"Nope," the man said, he looked bored and ready to

escape already.

"No reason why I needed to drive an hour to come in here to get this? It isn't normal practice, or did something change?"

The woman shrugged and looked at Cupert.

He rolled his eyes, "Just doing what we're told. We don't make the rules, just enforce them."

"Humph, okay then. Thanks." Ryder spun on her heel and headed toward the door.

"Y'all come back and see us sometime now, ya' hear." The woman's voice rang out and stopped Ryder in her tracks. She looked over her shoulder and saw the brunette's big bubbly grin. Cupert snickered behind her back, earning a smack from the woman.

"Sure," she said noncommittally, and slid through the doors as they swooshed open in front of her. "I think they've been out in the wild too long," she murmured, as the doors closed behind her.

Hopping into her Jeep, she took a few seconds to look at her permit. The itinerary was printed on it; along with advisories for the area she would be in. The thing that thrilled her most—her name across the bottom: Sparks, Ryder.

She couldn't stop the squeal that escaped her lips. Revving up the Jeep, she tore out of the parking lot. One more week and she would be on the trip of a lifetime.

CHAPTER TWO

March 16 – 0800

Ryder sat in her parents' living room and checked the contents of her backpack one last time. "Dad, did you put that sunscreen in my bag? I'm not seeing it."

Her dad emerged from the kitchen with a cup of coffee in one hand and the sunscreen in the other. "You know we don't drive up there until tomorrow, right?"

"Yeah, but I wanted to make sure everything was ready to go today." She spun in a circle; mentally checking items off her list. Logically, she knew she had everything, but this was her first big solo trip. The first time she wouldn't have her overprotective father and her *pack-everything-under-the-sun* mother. The first time she couldn't turn to one of her brothers and borrow gear, if by chance she didn't have it with her.

Her dad dropped the bottle of sunscreen on the couch next to her first aid kit. "And you couldn't do that at your place?"

Ryder looked up at his amused face and scrunched her

nose. "Pansy said if I unpacked and repacked the bag one more time, she was going to toss it out the window."

He snorted and sat down on the only available piece of furniture. Ryder had spread out everything she was taking, and it covered the couch, the recliner — reclined back for more space of course — and the coffee table.

After cataloguing everything in her head, she methodically began repacking the bag. There was a science to getting the most out of the pack she would be taking. Her sleeping bag was compressed and in the bottom. The center was for water, a water filter, food, and cooking gear. The sides and top would have her clothing, tent components, and other light or compressible items. And, last but definitely not least, the lid would have a map, snacks, and other essentials: lip balm and sunscreen. Bottles of water would also be placed in the outer pockets, and she could stick her walking poles next to the waters, and secure them with straps near the top of the pack.

It didn't take her long to get everything back inside just the way she wanted. It was a good thing too. Her little brother Jonathan — if you could call a six-foot tall, twenty-one-year-old little — came sluggishly down the stairs and flopped on the now empty couch. "Do you have to make so much noise this early in the morning?" he groused, flinging an arm across his eyes.

"Shouldn't you be dressed for work, son?"

Jon grunted in reply.

"I'd take that as a no, dad," Ryder said. "Maybe you should dock his pay." She snickered and closed up the recliner, then set her pack next to it. Walking past Jon, she stabbed him in the bottom of his foot with her finger. He bolted upright and glared at her.

"Brat," he said.

"Jerk," she replied, sticking her tongue out at him. She went into the kitchen and poured a cup of coffee. A dollop of creamer later, she headed back into the living room and sat in the recliner.

"Too much to drink last night, baby brother?" She smirked over the rim of her cup, as Jon's eyes rounded in surprise. She knew he'd gone out with his friends the night before. Pansy made a point of telling her they'd shown up at the bar she worked at. It would totally piss their dad off too, especially since Jon would be filling in for her at the store while she was on vacation.

"Son," their dad said in that deep 'you better tell the truth or I'm gonna beat your ass' voice.

Ryder loved to see her brothers get in trouble. She considered it payback for being overprotective dicks while in high school. Sure, it was great they had her back, but they made it damn near impossible to date. It hadn't been until her junior year that she had her first boyfriend, and she only got to date him because he was new to the school. He hadn't been warned to stay away or had his manhood threatened when her brothers were still there.

When Jonathan was a freshman and she was a senior, he picked up right where her two older brothers, Cameron and Nathan, left off. Thankfully, by that time she had a pretty steady boyfriend. They stayed together until after graduation, when he took off for college on the other side of the country, and she stayed there in Flagstaff. She wasn't heartbroken; and last she'd heard, he'd gotten married and had a kid on the way.

Jon grimaced. "Sorry, dad. I was just hanging with the guys. Shawn's girlfriend broke up with him, so we were helping cheer him up." His green eyes turned toward her in irritation. "How did you know I went out?"

"Oh please, you went to Frontier's."

"So what. I could have gone there for dinner."

Ryder snorted. *Like that would ever happen.* "Pansy works there, freak. She told me all about your drinking and singing karaoke like you were some dried up pop star. Who do you think poured you into the cab to get home?"

13

"She needs to mind her own business," he grumbled.

"It's a good thing she didn't," their dad remarked. "Get your ass up and ready for work. I'm going to guess you forgot you were covering for your sister today, as well as the rest of the week."

Jon groaned and let his head drop onto the back of the couch. "Who decides to make a backcountry trip in mid-March?"

Ryder knocked back the rest of her coffee and stood. "I do. Especially when they open up the season a little early, and we've got a friend that gave me the heads up. I can't wait to get started."

Their dad set his cup on the table and stood. Plucking her cup from her hand, he placed it next to his before enveloping her in a hug. He dropped a kiss on her head, then held her at arm's length. "You're going to leave your pack here and I'll bring it. Lord knows Pansy will probably kill you if you go through it again. Pop by the store later. I should be getting a shipment of the Jetboil stoves in. I want you to take one and try it out. You can give a review of it to our customers."

She grinned happily. "Sure thing. I'll come by in the afternoon." It was pretty great her family owned a sporting and outdoors store. She had the latest and greatest equipment at her fingertips whenever she wanted. Not that she got as many chances to use them as Nate did. Field-testing the products was something she secretly hoped to get into more. She just hadn't gotten the nerve to talk to her dad about it.

"Drake, you can lecture her later while you drive her to the trail head. We need to get going so we can open the store." Ryder's mom, Julie, came gliding down the stairs. She was dressed in cute brown cargo pants, snazzy bright green sneakers, and a Sparks Sporting & Outdoors shirt.

Ryder was a carbon copy of her mother: five-foot four inches in height, and both weighed around one hundred and twenty pounds. They each sported short, springy brown hair and dazzling — according to her father — green eyes. They were short and pixie-like on the outside, but tough as nails on the inside.

Her mom breezed through the living room with a brief stop to kiss Ryder on the cheek. She eyed her youngest, eyebrow raised and stern look on her face. Jonathan got up without a word and kissed their mom before heading upstairs. "See ya' later, brat."

"Whatever, jerk." She went to grab her pack, but her dad stopped her.

"Nope. Leave it. I know you too well, Ryder; you'll go through it five more times if it's within reach. I'm saving your life by keeping it here."

Ryder laughed and hugged her dad quickly. "See ya' later." Spinning she left the house and climbed into her Jeep. What the hell should she do now? It didn't take her long to make up her mind. Reversing out of her parents' driveway, she took off toward her favorite bakery. It was the first day of her vacation and she deserved a sweet treat.

CHAPTER THREE

March 17 – 0800

Ryder bounced in her seat waiting for her dad to come out of the house. She'd wanted to leave earlier, but he put the kibosh on that. Something about him being too old to get up with the chickens. Ryder thought it had more to do with the fact that he liked sleeping in, thanks to her older brothers taking a bigger role in running the store.

She was surprised when Jonathan strolled out the front door and made a beeline for her Jeep. He pulled open the passenger door and climbed inside without a word.

"What are you doing?"

"Dad is making me come along so I can talk to you while we head up. He and Mom are going to follow." He clipped his seatbelt in and leaned the chair back as far as it could go. Closing his eyes, he crossed his arms over his chest and promptly dozed off.

Minutes later their parents came out of the house. Their dad rapped on the windshield, making Jon bolt up and choke on the seatbelt. Ryder laughed as he sputtered and flailed. Her little brother never ceased to amuse her.

Jon raised his seat and glared out the front window after their parents climbed into the truck next to them.

"You know you can go back in if you want. I don't need you to come with me."

"Yeah you do," he grumped and slumped in the seat.

"You're such a brat sometimes," she said, letting her fondness for her younger sibling leak through.

Backing out of the driveway, she pulled forward and waited for her parents to follow suit. The plan was for them to follow her to the Backcountry Information Center where she would drop her car off. At that point, she would get in their truck and they would take her to the Grandview Trailhead, about twelve miles east of Grand Canyon Village. After four to five days of hiking the trails, she would take the free park shuttle bus from South Kaibab Trailhead back to the village and her Jeep.

It was a well thought out plan, at least in her opinion. She'd read about this particular trek on a website, and knew it was the one for her. According to the website, not too many people took this particular route. There were limited water sources, but enough that she would be able to refill and purify her own stock when she got low. The temperatures and conditions varied, but with the recent good weather, she knew it wouldn't be bad. There might be some icy and snow-covered stretches in the beginning, but it should clear out the further she hiked. She had a pair of microspikes packed just in case. Those, along with her poles, should get her through any sketchy areas.

It was the perfect trip to catch some alone time and let her mind roam free.

Caught up in her own thoughts, it took her a second to realize Jon was talking to her.

"Yo, Ryder. You in there?"

"Huh?" She glanced at him quickly, and then focused back on the road. They had an hour and a half trip ahead of them, and she didn't want something to go wrong before she even arrived there. Well, she didn't want anything to go wrong at all, but she learned never to expect things to be perfect. *Prepare for the worst, hope for the best*, was the family motto.

"I asked if you really knew what you were doing with this trek."

She shrugged to cover up the nervousness that bubbled in her tummy. She knew they were all concerned but, damn, she was tired of the over-protective hovering her family tended to do. "Yeah. I'm about as prepared as a girl can be."

"I don't know why you couldn't have waited a couple weeks when the weather was warmer, and I had some time coming to me."

"Ahhh, baby brother, are you concerned for your big sister?"

"Shut up," he said lightly. "I only wanted to come along so I could relax."

"You know this is a five-day trek I'm trying to squeeze into four. I plan on seeing the sights and busting my ass."

"Yeah, but at night when you're under the stars and just hanging out…"

"I'll be too tired to notice," she laughed.

"Nah, not you. You're practically vibrating in your seat to get out there. You'll hike all day, and then drink in the peace of the night. I have to say, I'm a little jealous."

That surprised her. Ever since she decided to take this trip last year, she'd gotten nothing but flack from everyone, well, except her mom that is. Her mom understood she needed this. Needed to try something on her own and get in touch with nature. They were both that way. They were out of sync with life if they didn't get out there and enjoy it. Problem was they tended to do it as a family or big group.

"You're probably right," she admitted. "But I need this time alone." She felt her brother's gaze zoned in on her. "Not that I don't love you guys and all, but I need a break from you people."

Jon chuckled just like she knew he would. "You people? That's harsh, sis."

Ryder couldn't help but roll her eyes at that. "I'm not saying anything you don't already feel. If you had this chance to be on your own, you'd go for it in a heartbeat."

While she may be closer in age to Nathan, him being only two years older, as opposed to Jon's three years younger; they had never really been close. He and Cameron treated her like she was a pest. They ditched her every opportunity they could. When Jonathan came into the world, Ryder had been thrilled. She was disappointed that he wasn't a girl, but that didn't stop her from making him play with her when he got out of that icky baby stage. She was pretty sure there was a picture of a two-year-old Jonathan in a dress with make-up on; done lovingly by five-year-old Ryder, which their mom was holding on to in order to humiliate him in front of any girl he got serious with. The serious girlfriend had yet to happen, but her mother held out hope.

Jon sighed and scrunched down into the seat some more. He looked like the brooding teen she remembered him to be not too many years ago. "You're right. You, Nate, and Cam are lucky you don't live at home any more. I wish the guys would let me move in with them."

Ryder couldn't help bursting out laughing. "That'll never happen. It's only a two-bedroom apartment. I don't think Nate or Cam are going to let you bunk in their bedrooms."

"Nate is almost never there. He spends more time at the parks than anywhere else. I wouldn't be surprised if he tracked you down while you are on your self-discovery adventure."

"He won't," she said smugly. "He's covering for one of his friends that works the guided tours. I think he's got Jeep tours today, tomorrow, and Thursday, then he's working the weekend doing the wagon trail rides."

"Awesome," Jon chuckled. "He hates those things."

They settled into a comfortable silence after that. The hour and a half whizzed by without incident. When they pulled up at the information center, she locked up the Jeep and tucked the keys into her pack, which she took from the house before her dad had a chance to tell her no. There was a small part of her that thought he would refuse to give the bag to her, thus killing her plans for the week.

Her parents pulled in a couple of spaces away and she and Jon started to walk over. He flung his arm across her shoulder and gave her a slight squeeze. "Have fun, brat. Make sure no critters get ya'."

"Thanks, jerk."

CHAPTER FOUR

March 17 – 1000

Ryder waved as her family pulled out of the parking lot, and she didn't stop until they disappeared around the corner. She knew she would only believe they'd left when she saw it with her own eyes.

After dropping her Jeep off, it took fifteen minutes to get to the Grandview Trailhead. Then, there had been another fifteen minutes of her mother and father fussing over her before they got back into their truck with her brother and drove off. They reminded her to be aware of every creature known to man, whether they would be out or not. Her father checked and rechecked her PBL, personal locator beacon. He then asked if she really wanted to go through with it, and offered to reimburse her the money she'd already spent on the permit and supplies.

She did her best not to roll her eyes at them, but Jon caught her a time or two.

He leaned back against the truck and laughed the entire time. On some level, he knew how it frustrated her when they treated her like a baby. What he didn't know was that it was actually beginning to wear on her. It was beginning to make her wish she had gone away to college or something. Found something else to do with her life that would take her away from the *only girl* madness.

One last look at the road, she took a deep breath and set off on the first leg of her trip. It was a four and a half to five mile rugged descent that would take her to her choice of campsites on Cottonwood Creek. The upper sections were still held together by logs and steel rods dating back to the days of the Last Chance Mine. During her research, she learned that some of the sections were filled with cobblestones in order to keep the trail level. It would be a bitch of a descent otherwise and definitely unsafe.

Once she made it down to Horseshoe Mesa, she would set camp beneath the red cliffs and lay down under a night sky peppered with stars. Or find a spot closer to the creek so she could listen to the water as it lulled her to sleep. Either one would be fantastic.

A couple hours went by and she was already feeling reenergized. She planned on stretching the hike out for as long as possible. The time away would do wonders for her soul. The cool air and ice beneath her feet, not to mention the full pack on her back as she descended made it a welcome challenge. She stopped briefly for water and to soak up the scenery before heading off again. In all, the first leg should only take her five hours at most.

A couple hours later, after multiple stops for pictures and a couple tight squeezes on the trail, she crossed The Saddle and closed in on Horseshoe Mesa. The ruins of Pete Berry's cabin, the man that rebuilt the trail she'd just traversed, appeared and she paid her respects.

It took a little time, but she got to Cottonwood Creek and found a campsite. She pitched her tent near some scrub to help provide protection and decided to grab a quick meal.

Exhausted from her day, she tucked herself in for the night. A sense of accomplishment flowed over her and her eyelids closed. Five miles down a treacherous path, and it had been fairly smooth sailing. She couldn't wait for the next day.

Ryder let the sound of bubbling water lull her to sleep. A wolf howled in the distance, calling to her. Welcoming her home.

CHAPTER FIVE

March 18 – 0600

Ryder stretched and waited to see how much of her body was sore. Her back snapped, crackled, and popped with each move. Her calves tightened and screamed as they bunched up. Bolting upright, she grabbed her toes and tried to make the cramp go away. "Ow, ow, ow," she chanted until the pain began to recede.

Flopping back, she exhaled a huge relieved breath. "Holy mother of God that sucked." Feeling around the sleeping bag, she blindly searched for her watch. The cold of the metal seeped into her hand as she gripped it and brought it her face. Six AM "Like clockwork."

In this one instance, it was great for her since she needed every minute of the day for this trip. First up on the agenda would be using the chemical toilet near the main camping area.

Slipping on a pair of shorts and shoes, she grabbed her light coat and pulled it on over the shirt she'd slept in. There wasn't anyone around to care if she wore the same thing.

Unzipping the tent's flap, she crawled out and sucked in a huge breath of fresh morning air. Stretching she glanced around. As expected, there weren't any other hikers that came in during the night. Her solo trip was still blissfully solo.

Trudging off to the toilet, she found she was surprised her brothers hadn't shown up during the night. She wouldn't have put it past them to ruin her trip. They still saw her as the little high school kid that needed protecting. They refused to believe she could take care of herself.

Ten minutes later Ryder was back in her tent slathering on hand sanitizer before gathering up her filtered water bottles. There wouldn't be many opportunities to fill up, and she knew to take advantage when she could, especially since her calves cramped up earlier. She would need to stay hydrated to avoid that again.

She zipped her tent back up, made sure her permit was still nestled away in the plastic bag dangling from the top, and took off for the creek. It didn't take her long to reach the edge of the water. Carefully she stepped out onto a rock, crouching down with her first bottle. The water rushed by with bits of debris floating on top, she discovered if she stepped out onto a small pile of rocks, she'd have an easier time filling up the bottles and less chance of foreign matter. Making quick work of moving further into the stream, she hummed a soft tune until she was done with her task. She clipped the bottles onto the waistband of her shorts and stood.

The scenery around her was beautiful. Red clay walls jutted up from the ground. Soft morning light touched the shrubbery and glinted off the water. There was a slight chill to the air, but it wasn't intolerable. It was crisp and fresh. It tingled her lungs as she inhaled and made her feel alive.

She turned to make her way back to the water's edge when a figure down stream, partly hidden by scrub, snagged her attention. It was crouching…no, *its on four legs*. Her brain scrambled to make sense of what she was seeing. The chance of running into a wild animal was slim, especially for this area. With typical human traffic the animals tended to stay away, even when the area was out of season.

Squinting she tried to figure out what it was. Definitely not human, not the way it was crouched in the water, and definitely not a deer or elk. The figure was too bulky, like it was filled out with long fur. There wasn't a rack on the creature's head either.

It turned in profile and its ears twitched, perking up. *A stray dog?* No, that couldn't be right. There weren't any reports of stray or wild dogs in the area. She'd checked before coming out. Not only was that common sense, but also the last thing she felt like enduring was a lecture on animal attack preparation from her father and know-it-all brothers.

The animal waded around the water before taking a drink. Like her, it moved into the middle of the icy water, though it was seemingly unaware she stood upstream from it. It was odd that he didn't notice her. Wolves were keen hunters and well aware of their surroundings. To let a human this close was unheard of.

Slowly, Ryder inched forward, inexplicably drawn to the creature. There was a noble, almost powerful aura around him. Like he knew he was the king of his domain and all that entered it. Common sense told her to turn around and leave as quietly as possible. Her father's voice rang through her head, telling her to stop right that minute.

Ryder's foot slipped slightly. Slick green algae had formed on the rocks embedded in the creek bed. One wrong step and she'd end up alerting her wolf she was coming toward him. She glanced down quickly to check her intended path, then back up at her wolf. He waded further downstream, oblivious to her. Not wanting to lose him, she picked up her pace; gradually making her way to the opposite side of the creek she started on.

Regardless of everything her family harped on, she wasn't backing away. All her life she'd been in love with wolves. Unlike the other kids who flocked to the tigers and lions at the zoo, she'd made a beeline for the wolf enclosure. They called to her on an elemental level and sang to her soul. While she could sit for hours watching them, wishing to be part of their pack, her heart broke at their captivity and inability to do whatever they wanted. At the zoo they were dependant on their keepers and the schedule they were forced to bow down to.

Wolves had an appetite for freedom. They needed to follow the wind and let their instincts guide them. They were intelligent and focused. Just once she'd love to feel what it would be like to be one. This handsome ash-colored wolf was her one chance to experience a tiny bit of it.

Slowly — methodically, she made her way closer. It was strange to see him alone in the water. Wasn't he concerned about being caught unaware?

Hopefully his pack isn't too far away. She would hate for someone to harm him because he was alone.

Ryder quickly stopped in her tracks. Whoa! If there were more, her ass might be in trouble. *"Don't let the critters get ya',"* Jon's voice echoed in her head. Even now they wouldn't leave her alone.

Glancing around, she didn't see any other movement. There were no other wolves that she could see hanging around waiting for their Alpha. No other wolf joined him in the water or waited for him on the banks.

Letting out a slow breath, she took a few more steps forward. She was so close now. Within twenty-five feet of him. He was magnificent and massive compared to her, probably standing a good four feet at the shoulder. Adding in his head, he would be able to look her almost in the eyes. Ryder gulped and cursed her mother's genes for making her short.

Her foot slipped, splashing in the water. The animal's

head whipped in her direction, and his golden yellow eyes stood out against his dark face, zeroing in on her.

She froze in her tracks. "Shit," she squeaked.

Crouching, the animal stalked toward her. Head down. Eyes glued to her.

Her heart went into overdrive, beating a rapid tattoo against her chest. She thought the damn thing would burst free if given the chance. Panic swiftly overtook all thoughts, yet she couldn't move. Her body refused to listen to her brain, which was screaming…*run*.

As the animal got closer, she numbly realized she was getting that look she was determined to have. It was everything she thought it would be. Power and strength oozed off of him. She wanted to call to him and beg him to let her bask in his glory. There had to be something seriously wrong with her to think that. The animal would never let her run her fingers through his thick, luxurious coat as he idly sat by. He'd more than likely want to gobble her up Little Red Riding Hood style.

Suddenly, he stopped in his tracks just ten feet away. His large dark head cocked to the side, black snout thrust up as he sniffed the air.

Ryder shivered in reaction. She knew exactly what he was doing. He could smell her on the light breeze. Scent her excitement, nervousness, and panic. "Oh God, please tell me I don't stink," she whispered.

His head dropped down and he started forward again. That's when her limbs unlocked and decided to heed the brain's warning. Controlling the urge to run — barely — she slowly stepped back, eyes locked on the beast. Cold water splashed against her skin, but she didn't care. The corners of his wolfy mouth pulled back, showing off sharp, white, gleaming teeth. If she didn't know any better, she would have said he was smiling, pleased at her retreat and looking forward to the chase. But that couldn't be true because wolves didn't smile. Wolves didn't read your thoughts or talk out loud. They weren't human. They growled and sneered. They threatened and looked as if they were ready to eat you.

Abruptly, the silly grin that couldn't be one, disappeared and he stopped moving completely. His gaze dropped to her foot, pulling her own gaze down with it. A precarious pile of slick rocks lay right where her foot was headed. There was no stopping what was about to happen, so she braced for impact. Little did she know, it wouldn't do her any good.

Dread filled his stomach as the cuter than hell pixie, who smelled like heaven, stepped back onto a pile of wet rock protruding from the water. There was nothing he could do to stop the accident about to happen.

Sure, he could lunge for her and capture her in his teeth. Or shift while in mid-air and attempt a save. That one would mean exposing himself in more than one way. He wasn't prepared to have to explain who and what he was. Humans, in general, didn't take the knowledge of shifters well.

When he'd gotten a good whiff of her earlier, he'd noted no shifter pheromones at all. A healthy dose of feminine musk that he wanted to lick off every inch of her delectable little body, but no shifter scent.

She squeaked in surprise as her foot landed, her arms flailed, and instead of pitching forward, like he'd hoped she'd do so she could catch herself, she tipped backwards into the creek. There was a splash, quickly followed by a grunt of pain, then nothing. She didn't scream or scramble to get back up. Water settled around her, rippling as it went past, and he caught the diluted coppery scent of blood.

Shit. She was basically dead in the water.

NO! Not dead. That would be bad.

What the hell was he supposed to do? There shouldn't

29

have been anyone out on the trails yet. It wasn't April, when the traffic around the area picked up. He should have had two more weeks out in the wild.

Fuck, he hated humans at times. They were always doing shit they shouldn't, like camping out of season because they didn't think they had to abide by the rules.

Sighing in resignation, because it didn't look like she would be waking up anytime soon, he padded over to where she fell. Gideon looked down at her lovely heart-shaped face, immediately enchanted by what he saw. Short brown hair rode the ripples of water around her head. Her cherry lips were parted slightly and her face relaxed, it looked as if she were merely taking a nap. He didn't know if he wanted to nudge her awake so he could see what color her eyes were, or if he should curl up next to her to soak in her scent.

Whoa there, buddy. We aren't curling up next to anyone.

The wolf yipped his displeasure, then moved a little closer. He pressed his snout into her neck. Grazed his teeth along her collarbone. Gideon barely stopped the beast from marking her with his bite, claiming her for himself.

Hell no! You have got to be shitting me. The human protested inside, forcing the wolf to step back. They needed space between them and the girl, who was apparently his mate. *Fuck!*

This was the last thing he wanted after his nasty break-up a couple weeks ago. Nicole had been furious with him when he called it all off, instead of making her his Luna. She gave him an ultimatum, and he'd picked the option that best suited him. She wasn't his mate and he wasn't about to pretend otherwise. He wasn't interested in finding a new ladylove. Not now, maybe not ever. Playing the field was all he could handle at the moment.

The wolf huffed out a breath in aggravation, clearly not agreeing. Lowering his muzzle close to her face again, he noted she was breathing just fine. He nudged her chin with his nose, hoping to rouse her. Her head lolled slightly to the side, but those pretty lashes lay unmoving.

Blood oozed into the water, catching his attention again. *Fuck, she's hurt.*

His wolf whimpered, wanting to get down onto his stomach in the frigid water and crawl next to her. *Not happening buddy. That's some fucking cold ass water.*

Another wolf trotted up to him, bumping into his side. Gideon swiftly moved over her body, baring his teeth and growled.

His beta, Diego, took a couple steps back.

The mental connection between them snapped into place, and Diego's voice entered his head.

Gideon?

Mine, he snarled back, unable to stem the fierce possession he felt.

Diego's wolf took a couple more steps back before shifting. He held out his hands to show he meant no harm, leaving his naked body vulnerable. "Alpha, I mean no harm to her."

She's hurt. It was a blessing within his Pack that they were able to keep the connection between them in whatever form they were. It was more efficient for them all not have to shift back and forth just to have a conversation.

"You need to get her out of the water, Gideon. I'll stay back. She needs your help."

Logically he knew that. A small niggle of guilt formed in the back of his mind. He'd known she was there filling up her water. He'd smelled a barely there scent of roses that had him edging toward her before he caught himself. He didn't perceive any threat from her. In fact, she appeared too preoccupied with getting her own drink to notice him. As a precaution, he made a point to stick behind the scrub as much as possible. With his dark coat, it should have been easy for him to blend in. Apparently not.

She'd seen him and, instead of running away, she moved toward him. He didn't know if it was stupidity or innate curiosity that gave her courage. He sure as hell would find out, as soon as he got her to safety.

Stepping to the side, he placed himself between Diego and the woman his wolf wanted to claim. Gideon shook himself like a dog to release the tension knotting him, preparing for the change. Like the flip of a switch, he unleashed the power within that would start his transformation. Warm air swirled around him, and a fine mist formed at his feet. Bones popped and reshaped. Muscles stretched and flexed. Fur and claws receded, his teeth changed. It took only a matter of seconds.

He stretched his arms over his head and loosened the kinks in his back. He'd been in his wolf form for a couple days, and hadn't planned to change back until he was damn good and ready. Usually, he would get home, shower up, then see their healer or her apprentice for a bone melting massage. There wouldn't be time for that now. Even though he'd leashed his wolf, the beast continued to prowl beneath the surface. The worry over his mate lying still in the cold water made Gideon's very human guilt flare.

Diego cleared his throat. "You okay there?"

Gideon looked to his oldest friend and frowned. How could he possibly be okay with any of this? "What do you think?"

"Okay. You aren't happy. I can see that. What are you going to do? It isn't like you can shift back and walk away. Your wolf won't let you."

Gideon's eyebrow rose imperiously. He could do whatever the hell he wanted, to include leaving his mate in the cold creek bed to possibly die of hypothermia.

"Yeah, yeah, you can; but you won't. She's your mate, I'm guessing, based on that little dominating display, and she's hurt." They both looked down at the woman in the water. Her lips were starting to turn a bluish-purple. The color leeched from her face.

"How did she get hurt in the first place? Did you find her like that?"

There was no stopping the heat racing across Gideon's cheeks. "No," he growled between clenched teeth. "She spotted me and started coming toward me. I thought I would scare her off by stalking toward her. Unfortunately, that plan backfired when she slipped on some rocks and…" his words trailed off as he motioned to her.

The breeze picked up at that moment. As hot as he usually ran, his skin pebbled with goose bumps as cold air brushed past him. He needed to make a decision; one he hoped he didn't regret. He squeezed his eyes shut and gave the order that would, no doubt, change his entire life. "Head back to the compound. Have my room stripped and readied for our arrival. We'll need fresh meat and clothes for her. Once that's taken care of bring a truck. I'll find her campsite and get her looked over and warmed up. She should be ready to travel by the time you make it back. We'll meet at the Grandview Trail head."

"Of course, Alpha. Is there anything else?"

There would be so much more; but for now, he needed to get her out of the water and safely installed in his home. Like it or not, he'd found his mate. His *human* mate.

"No. Not right now. Keep this to yourself for the time being. I don't need it to get out that I've found my mate. Not before I've had a chance to talk to her. I don't need her freaking out and end up with a wolf chasing her tail."

Diego stepped forward and cuffed him on the shoulder. "The Fates know what they're doing. It'll work out, Gideon. Things happen for a reason."

Gideon snorted. "Says the man who actually *wants* to find his mate."

"We're not pups anymore. It's time to grow up and settle down. The Pack needs it."

Gideon answered that bit of advice with a growl.

Diego's amused laughed died away as he shifted to wolf. The large black beast loped off through the woods, headed back to the Keystone Predator compound. Once he was out of sight, Gideon released a breath and focused on his newest problem.

His pixie needed out of the ball-freezing water, and he needed to plain ole cover his ass. Bending down, he scooped up the woman; not at all surprised there was little weight to her. Not even the drenched fleece jacket wrapped around her torso weighed her down.

Fucking hell, she's fragile. She looked young too. Younger than he thought his mate would be. How could she possibly be strong enough to help him lead the Pack?

Tucked away in his arms, a sense of rightness flooded his system, throwing his world into disarray. His wolf howled in triumph at the feel of her body pressed against his. It pushed at him, rippling beneath the surface, demanding to be let loose. His vision wavered as his eyes bounced between man and wolf. The human side of him fought back, exerting his dominance over the beast this one time. It didn't take much for the wolf to back down. It was content being near her, just as the human side was. Gideon was royally fucked.

CHAPTER SIX

March 18 – 0700

Trudging up the bank with his shivering prize in his arms, it didn't take Gideon long to find her campsite. The rose-scented trail he associated with her, led him to a lone tent sitting snuggled up against a large swath of scrub brush. The dark green fabric of her shelter blended into the scenery nicely. If not for the scent and the baggie with what he assumed contained her permit clipped to the top, he might not have noticed it.

Pride filled his chest at seeing how clever she'd been. His pride didn't outweigh the anger swirling in the pit of his stomach knowing she was out there alone. There were no other hints of human or shifter. No fellow travelers scattered around that could help if she encountered a problem. What would she have done if people with the wrong intentions came upon the site and found her? Would she have been able to fend them off? He looked down at her again. No, he didn't think so. She was a petite woman, probably no taller or stronger than any of the young teens in the Pack.

His wolf rose, his teeth piercing his gums. He wanted to claim her, change her and make her theirs. The wolf didn't like Gideon's response of no. The woman would have the choice. Destined to be his mate or not, she would be the one to make the final decision.

Juggling her, the best he could, Gideon managed to unzip the end of what looked to be a two-man tent and crawled inside with her in his arms. He laid her out next to her sleeping bag, drumming up his courage to do what came next. He would need the warmth of the bag to raise her core temperature. The longer she stayed in those clothes, the colder she would get, and her internal organs would begin to fail.

Slipping her boots and socks off, he went to work on the way too tiny tan shorts plastered to her backside.

What the fuck is she doing wearing so little?

It was still cold out. Mid-March — the highs were around fifty-four degrees, and that was mid-to-late afternoon. This early in the morning, it couldn't be more than twenty-five out. She should have been covered head to toe in warm comfy layers. It should take him ages to peel every inch of clothing from her. To reveal her luscious little body to his hungry gaze bit by bit.

He groaned as he slid his hands, palms up, beneath her. Her ass fit perfectly in his grasp. He could already imagine holding the firm globes as she bounced on his cock, bringing them both pleasure. Her pert little breasts would bob up and down, tempting him.

Sucking in a steadying breath, he peeled the shorts down her silky smooth legs, snagging her itty-bitty panties with them. He forced his gaze to remain on her face in case she woke up and freaked the hell out. Tossing the drenched items in the corner of the tent, he maneuvered her to an upright position and took off the jacket and t-shirt she wore beneath. Her breasts were bare, damn near causing him to swallow his tongue. Her nipples were perked up, begging to be sucked and nibbled on like sweet cherries.

Shifting his focus, he took the time to assess the damage to her head. As gently as he could, he sifted his fingers through her hair, finding the bump with unerring accuracy. He parted the hair around it and ascertained it had stopped bleeding. It was red and angry, but the cut wasn't very deep. She'd have a hell of a headache when she woke, but that should be about it. A little rest and he didn't doubt she'd be back on her feet in no time.

Moving her onto her rumpled sleeping bag, he tucked her in carefully. A soft moan escaped her blue-tinged lips, earning a whimper from his wolf. He wanted to crawl in next to her to speed up the warming process. It was logical and probably recommended in lieu of a heated blanket.

Gideon debated a full five minutes about the pros and cons of that idea and, in the end, the cons may not have outweighed the pros, but the cons were pretty fucking big. It wasn't the way he wanted to start things off with his mate.

Fuck! I don't want a mate!

Scrambling out of the tent as quickly as he could, Gideon surveyed the area. He had the good fortune to discover she'd camped near his secret cache of clothes and supplies. Finding what he needed, he was gone and back within five minutes. Leaving his unconscious pixie longer than necessary was not an option, no matter how much he protested the idea of a mate. He slipped on the T-shirt and shorts that were inside the camouflage bag, leaving the socks, hiking boots, and everything else inside. He wouldn't need any of it anytime soon.

Turning to open the tent again, the bag with the permit flapped against the nylon top, as if calling to him. He unclipped and opened it, curious to find out her name. Waiting for her to wake up would take too long. At least that's what he told himself. Reaching in, he pulled out the neatly folded paper.

"Sparks, Ryder," he said out loud. "Damn, Sparks.

Why does that name sound familiar?" He tried to search through his memory to figure out where he'd heard the name before. It hadn't been in passing, he was sure. It had been Donna, one of the pack members, that'd brought it up at a recent gathering. The first name hadn't been Ryder though. It had been Nate. His gaze was drawn to the opening of the tent. He hoped like hell that wasn't her husband.

His wolf's growl broke through his chest.

"Married? Fuck that," he whispered fiercely. The desire to dive back inside and shake her awake rocked him. He needed to know if she was married. If she were, she'd have a hard time explaining she was mated to a wolf, and not some simpering human when she broke it off.

Taking a deep breath, Gideon scanned the permit again looking for an answer to one of his earlier questions, giving himself a couple of much-needed seconds to compose himself.

"I guess they opened the season early. Fuck! Donna should have told us before we took off."

Ryder was clearly within the parameters of the dates listed on the itinerary. There were two more nights listed on the slip of paper. She was certainly a determined woman if she thought she could turn a five-day hike into a long four days.

Gideon stuffed the paper in the baggie before hooking it back to the tent. His wolf tugged at him to join her, needing to touch her. Who was he to resist at the moment? The cold had seeped into his bones while emotional exhaustion dragged him down.

Kneeling, he unzipped the tent and started to crawl back inside. Ryder was still flat on her back in the sleeping bag, exactly as he'd left her. He realized a little too late there was one huge difference. Her eyes were barely open and drilling a hole into him.

Ryder watched through narrowed eyes as a man made his way into her tent. She knew she should be terrified, *had* been when she realized where she was, and that she was completely naked. She'd quickly grabbed the pepper spray near the head of the sleeping bag and clutched it tightly in her fist.

She'd listened, rigid with fear, as a growl rent the air seconds before the tent had been unzipped. A dark swath of hair entered her line of sight first and instead of her panic increasing, she mentally noted his hair was a bit long on top. Enough that she could thread her fingers through it, and feel the silky strands against her palms. As he looked up, deep brown eyes with flecks of gold made contact with hers, and her anxiety mysteriously melted. The knots in her stomach vanished as though they had never even been there. Her body immediately relaxed into the cocoon of her sleeping bag and her eyes shut.

"I see you're awake," he said, his deep voice taking on a hesitant edge. There was a question ringing through his words. Like he wanted to make sure it was okay for him to still come in. She had a feeling he would whether she wanted him to or not. When she didn't say anything, she assumed he took her non-answer for the answer, as he crawled the rest of the way inside before closing off the world again. The sound of the tent zipping back up thrummed against her ears.

"What happened?" she muttered. Her body quaked, as a sharp needle-like pain ripped through her skull. The last thing she remembered was a huge handsome wolf coming toward her, grinning like she was its next meal.

She heard him shift things around; she'd guess, in an attempt to get comfortable. There wasn't much room in her tent, despite the fact it was designed for two people. She tended to spread out when she camped. Never having to share with her brothers when they got older, it became habit. Briefly she thought about scooting over, but knew it would involve moving…and letting a complete stranger snuggle up next to her. *Which sounds so good right now. No it doesn't*, she reprimanded herself.

"You slipped in the creek and smacked your head pretty good," he said, his voice pitched low and close to her ear. Heat emanated from him, making her want to wiggle closer.

"Really, you mean I wasn't run over by a Mack truck all the way out here?"

He snorted and she smiled. She could picture the look on his face. One corner of his mouth would curve up into a sexy half grin. Those soulful brown eyes would twinkle with delight.

Sexy? Come on girl, you barely got a look at him. Ha! She'd seen enough to know. Without a doubt, he would be sexy as sin once she could look at him without pain dulling her vision.

She cracked an eyelid open and peeked at him, turning her head slightly. She winced when she put pressure on what felt like a pretty good-sized bump. "*Motherfuck*," she whispered harshly, squeezing her eyes shut.

"Turn your head back," he grouched softly. The gentle scrape of his fingers against her forehead and into her hair surprised and soothed her. He continued to caress her face, running his fingers along her cheek and jaw. Delicious warmth spread over her starting at her head, beating back the pain radiating through it.

She sighed in relief. "Just trying to get a better look at my rescuer." She rolled her head gingerly, and was thankful when the throbbing pain stopped.

"How do you know I'm the one who saved you?"

"The only other being out here was the massive wolf I saw. Last I checked, they couldn't unzip tents or peel clothes off unconscious women."

"Wonderful. A smart ass," he mumbled.

She would have snorted at how put out he sounded, but that would have hurt her head. "So, about my clothes," she tried to ask without actually asking. She could safely assume they hadn't been ripped from her body by a sudden raging river. The creek had a decent flow from melting snow, but it hadn't been anywhere near deadly. Vaguely, she wanted to know if he'd liked what he saw. *Quit thinking dumb shit. You don't know him.*

His fingers drifted away, and she mourned the loss of his touch. The pain slowly started back up. "You were soaked to the bone. I don't know what the hell you were doing out there with so little on. You may as well have been naked," his growl at the end had her stiffening. Her defenses went up and anger at his words burned through her.

Regardless of the pain multiplying by the second, she turned her head toward him. He was stretched out next to her, filling the space. Their faces were close, but not close enough that she could purse her lips and kiss him. His jaw clenched and eyes narrowed. Holy shit, he was actually pissed off.

"Listen mister," she started, but was abruptly cut off.

"Gideon," he corrected her through clenched teeth. His eyes flashed gold for a split second, but she couldn't be sure that was what she'd seen. The headache forming and resonating pain had to be playing tricks on her.

"Listen, Gideon, I'm not dressed…"

"Not anymore," he smirked. With those words, she was proven right. The corner of his mouth curved up into a devastating smile. His eyes did indeed twinkle, but with mischief not delight. *Maybe he did like what he saw.* As ridiculous as it should be, the thought sent a thrill through her. She wouldn't be letting him know.

Ryder schooled her features. "I'm not dressed any less than any other hiker that comes out into the backcountry."

"Maybe in late Spring."

41

"Would you stop interrupting me?"

"Nope. Not when I see a flaw in your logic."

She hastily pushed up and he followed, their gazes locked for precisely two seconds. "Argh! Men! You sound just like my brothers. Nate is always giving me a hard time about the clothes I wear. Just because he thinks he's *Mister Outdoors Extraordinaire*; it doesn't give him the right to criticize me. Shit, if he's so concerned about what women wear, maybe he should become a fashion designer." If it hadn't been for her head swimming and the need to rant, she would have realized her mistake immediately when she sat up. The sleeping bag slid down her torso baring her naked chest. Her nipples reacted, puckering in the cool air. Gideon's gaze slipped from her face for a reason. The flash of gold she wasn't sure she'd seen earlier — appeared again, and it didn't disappear. The longer she sat there, the brighter they became.

"Um, your eyes?"

When a growl broke free from his lips, she hastily scrambled to cover up. As she pulled the material back up, she glanced at Gideon. Pure unadulterated lust was painted across his face. His jaw flexed and nostrils flared. His glowing gaze trailed up her body, leaving fire in its wake and a ball of lust zinging straight to her belly. The air in the tent thickened with the smell of her arousal. Their gazes collided, and she made a startling revelation about the man next to her.

She blinked a couple of times, as her mind untangled the information sitting right in front of her. The wolf had been the only one around. No one could have gotten to her and scared him off in the time she'd smacked her head and gotten knocked out. He would have been on her like white on rice. Nibbling on one of her thighs by the time another human being had shown up.

Gideon's dark hair resembled the shaggy coat of the wolf. His eyes glowed a bright gold just as the wolf's eyes had. And the kicker — Gideon's feral smile was exactly like the one the wolf tossed in her direction as she tried to retreat from him. "You're my wolf. The one I saw out there."

Gideon stiffened, his eyes narrowing slightly. When he laid down on his side, propping his head up with his hand, his casual act didn't fool her. "How did you make that leap?" He snorted as if she'd said the most foolish thing in the world.

"Why aren't you denying it?" She retorted.

"Werewolves don't exist."

"Oh please," she said and rolled her eyes. "Not the kind the movies portray, but shifters do exist. My roommate is one. If there can be a fox-shifter, there can damn well be a wolf-shifter."

His brows furrowed in confusion. "Why don't I smell her on you?"

"A-ha!" she exclaimed, and did a little dance in her head. It would have hurt too much to do one physically. Her head throbbed, reminding her she should probably take it easy, but the excitement of meeting a wolf-shifter was worth it.

Ryder beamed at Gideon as he shut down. His face morphed into a blank mask, his lips pinched together. She didn't mind. It gave her an excuse to openly check him out and, *holy hell,* he took her breath away and made her pulse skip a beat.

She did a couple of quick calculations based on the size of the tent and brother comparison, figuring he was around six feet tall. Lean, rippling muscles as well as dark hair covered his arms and legs. Not in a gross way, but in a *hell yeah he's a man* way. He had a trim, tapered waist, perfect to wrap her shorter legs around. The fact his t-shirt didn't lay directly against his chest told her he had hair there, and the thought of running her hands over it all made her fingers tingle.

She'd been instantly attracted to a guy before, but this felt like…more. Everything about him felt familiar, as though they'd known each other all of their lives. Which was as far from the truth as possible.

She'd 'known' him for all of ten minutes. She didn't know how long she'd been out or what he'd done to her while basically comatose. *Nothing and you know it,* the tiny voice in her head said.

She felt safe around him. Knew he would never hurt her intentionally. That he would protect her with his life if it came to that.

It was fucking weird.

She had the overwhelming notion she belonged to him — body and soul. The need to have him take her, make her his in every way, excited her beyond belief. Okay, maybe not right at the moment. Her head hurt and her ankle throbbed uncomfortably. She couldn't stop the grin forming on her face when she thought about what would happen when she felt better. That man was going to be hers.

If there was one thing she learned from Pansy, it was that shifters knew their mates on contact. Gideon hadn't run off screaming and for a lone wolf out in the woods, he should have done that by now. There was something keeping him there with her, and she had a sneaky suspicion she knew what it was. She was smart enough to know she'd have to wait for him to make the first move.

Growing up with three brothers would finally come in handy. They'd taught her a lot about men. They didn't like to be told what to do, what to think, or how they felt. Hopefully, Gideon wouldn't take his sweet ass time figuring all of that out.

She licked her lips and smiled innocently. His fall was going to be sweet.

"Fuck," he grunted, and rolled onto his back, flinging an arm over his eyes.

Unable to resist, she reached out, resting her hand on his arm. Heat blasted up and into her chest. Her nipples puckered even more, and she ached to feel of his hands on them. Or his mouth. His mouth would do nicely for sure. She could thread her fingers into his hair, making sure he hit all of the right spots. "Anything I can help you with?" She asked, her voice husky with arousal.

Ryder's warm hand on his arm sent a shockwave of familiarity along his nerve endings. The wolf had been correct in his need for her. The longer he stewed it over, the less it pissed him off. A tiny, pixie-like human named Ryder was his goddamn mate. He couldn't pinpoint when the human half of him accepted the truth. Maybe, deep down, he'd known from the start. All they had done was stare at each other silently. She didn't pressure him to say more. A rarity when it came to women, in his experience. She only smiled and his heart tripped. It was like the heavens opened up and shined down on him. Then, she had the nerve to lick those cherry-red lips after she took the time to look him up and down like he was a damn treat to be had.

I'll give her something to suck on.

Gideon groaned as the immature thought rippled through his brain. The wolf bumped against his skin, and he knew his eyes would be glowing. "I'm fine," he growled a bit roughly and her hand lifted. He wanted to yell at her to put it back, to touch him more. The loss immediately made him uncomfortable and edgy.

She grunted and he listened as she lay back down. The sound of the silky sleeping bag caressing her skin reminding him she was completely naked. Soft, delicate skin that begged to have his hands all over it.

"You don't sound fine to me. Hell, the way you keep groaning and growling over there, you'd think *you* were the one that took a tumble. I'm the one whose head hurts like hell, and now my fucking ankle is bothering me," she

45

groused.

With swiftness she probably couldn't fathom, Gideon whipped back the edge of the sleeping bag. He ignored her gasp, as he stared down at her body. How could he be so stupid not to check for other injuries? "What else hurts?"

He ghosted his hands over her arms and torso, wary of hurting her more. Her skin was too cool for his liking. "Gideon, stop." She batted him away, but he wouldn't be deterred.

"No. Tell me what else hurts." He hadn't noticed anything when he took her boots off. It was possible that now she was thawed out a little and blood flowed again, the injury appeared. He lifted one leg then the other, laying them gently on top of the bag. Her left ankle had turned an interesting shade of blue and was swollen. He cradled her foot in his hand, cursing himself a hundred shades of fool because he decided to prowl toward her. He'd done nothing but injure his mate.

Ryder sat up, covering her breasts with her crossed arms. Damn, he wished she hadn't done that. He'd ignored the feel of her skin beneath his palms, concentrating on identifying damage. Now that he'd catalogued every scrape, bruise, and hurt, he wanted to soak in her naked body. The soft curves he wanted to have against his hard muscles. The waxed pussy he couldn't help but notice…no matter how hard he tried not to. Beaded cherry nipples he wanted to pluck and pinch.

"Damn," she grumped, pulling him out of his musings. She reached out to touch her ankle and crinkled her button nose. "I didn't think it was that bad. What do you think the chances are it'll be healed up by tomorrow so I can finish my hike?"

Blood rushed to his ears, drowning out anything else she might have said. "You are not finishing this hike," he said through gritted teeth.

She scowled at him. "That isn't your decision to make."

46

"It damn well is! You're hurt."

"No thanks to you," she pouted.

Gideon had to reign in his exasperation at her thinking she could continue this hike. He cleared his throat and tried to reason with her. "I'm sorry, Ryder. I don't see that happening. I'd be surprised if you can walk on it after a couple days. This looks pretty bad."

He missed it when her eyes narrowed and lips compressed. "How do you know my name?" She tugged on her leg, but he wouldn't let go.

He shrugged. "I read your permit when I went to get my clothes. I didn't expect you to wake up that soon."

Her anger cleared quickly, as her mouth opened on a silent O, before turning into a pleased little grin. "Oh, well, okay then. I'm cool with that." She flopped back, not bothering to cover up. Her breasts bounced and his cock jerked. She was splayed out before him, begging him to take a bite.

Gideon swallowed hard and attempted to keep his mind on the most pressing issue. And that wasn't the raging hard-on in his shorts. "Doesn't this hurt like hell?"

Brilliant green eyes rested on his face. "Not really. The pain goes away when you touch me. I'm not feeling too bad right now."

That made sense. It also solidified the mate theory. Shifters couldn't soothe the pains of another by touch alone, especially a human, if they weren't mates. The only odd thing was that he hadn't claimed her by bite yet. He also hadn't sunk his cock into her tight pussy and released inside her. "Interesting," he murmured.

"I think so too, which is why it would be in my best interest for you to get naked and do some full body contact pain relief."

Gideon snorted and tucked her legs back into the

47

bag. He pulled the material up to cover her tempting little body. Damn, she didn't know how bad he wanted to slide in next to her and feel her against him.

"Come on Gideon," she purred, "you know you want to." She batted her long lashes at him, the corner of her mouth curving into a saucy grin.

Shit! He was a weak man. She took his being a shifter a lot better than he ever thought a human would. He was also man enough to admit, if only to himself, that he was beyond pleased with his future mate. She would make a fantastic Luna to sit by his side.

He rolled her onto her right side, careful of her damaged ankle, leaving space for him behind her. He yanked his t-shirt over his head, tossing it into the corner. He stood, hunched over and quickly stepped out of his shorts. He crawled into the sleeping bag behind her before she had a chance to get a good look at him.

Snaking an arm underneath her head and one around her waist, he gently tugged her back into his body.

She gasped and giggled. "Oh my! Are you happy to see me or what?"

"Not now Ryder. Pain relief," he said gruffly. "That's why I'm doing this."

She wiggled her sassy ass back into his groin, eliciting a tortured groan from him. "I bet that isn't all."

"It's all you're going to get."

Her breathing turned shallow, and he knew the warmth of his body against hers, combined with the relief from the pain of her injuries had her falling asleep. Just when he thought she'd drifted off, her soft voice echoed in his ears. "For now."

CHAPTER SEVEN

March 18 – 700pm

Ryder came awake slowly. A comforting heaviness cloaked her body. With her eyes still closed, she wiggled to get comfortable, instantly aware of the hard, hot body behind her. The events of the day bombarded her. The wolf. The fall. The super hot guy that made her feel like she'd found her home.

Blinking a couple of times, she realized she'd been asleep longer than planned. Darkness had invaded the tent, and the quiet of the evening settled around them.

This isn't what I'd planned. She should have been at her next campsite tucking in for the night after a quick meal, and more miles under her feet. A wave of depression welled over her, pinching her chest. Breath lodged in her lungs, and she found it hard to breathe. The heavy arm around her waist, tightened fractionally.

"Breathe, pixie." His words gusted against her hair. They released the air in her lungs, allowing her to take a shaky breath.

She sighed, trying to shake the sadness choking her. "My trip is over, isn't it?"

The gentle press of his lips to the back of her head had her shutting her eyes tight. An unwanted tear escaped, fell from her face.

"It is," Gideon whispered. There was a depth of emotion in those two simple words. As if he knew how much this trip meant to her and shared in her disappointment.

She took a couple seconds to grieve the failed solo expedition. She would never know if she could have done it on her own. Didn't think there would ever be an opportunity to try again. Releasing another breath, she tried to let it all go.

"Maybe you can try again," he said.

Hope flared but immediately went out. Her parents would never let her try it again. It didn't matter that she was twenty-four and living on her own. Once they found out what had happened, they would wrap her up in cotton and stick her in the back room of the store away from any and everything. Plus, if she and Gideon were mates, like she thought, would he really let her? "I doubt it," she mumbled grumpily.

"You doubt what?"

"Oh, that I'll get a chance to try again. My parents are going to freak because I got hurt. I wasn't even doing anything dangerous when it happened."

"Yes, you were," he grunted.

"No, I wasn't. I was filling my water bottles and taking in the scenery. Getting ready to start day two."

"And then you decided to get close to a wild animal. Who in their right mind thinks that isn't dangerous?"

"I only wanted a closer look," she pouted, knowing she was in the wrong, but refusing to admit it. "Wolves

50

usually take off when a human gets near. They don't look for a fight. It was going fine until you noticed me."

"I knew you were there the entire time. I figured you would be too busy to notice, and I stayed partly hidden." He sighed in obvious irritation. "I'm not your usual wolf, as you've discovered."

"Ain't that the truth," she huffed out.

Gideon grunted instead of saying anything else.

Silence descended on them. She didn't know what was going through his mind, but she couldn't think about anything other than how different he was from almost every person she knew. *A fucking wolf-shifter.* A bubble of hysteria formed, trying to break free. Oh — my — God, she was snuggled up, naked ass to naked crotch, to a man who could change into a wolf. Not in her wildest dreams did she think this would ever happen to her. Her thoughts raced, never landing on one thing in particular, when he spoke.

"We're mates, Ryder." The way he said it made her think he wasn't pleased.

Regardless, his claim on her rasped over her senses, sending a shudder through her body she was barely able to suppress. The idea of him claiming her made her lightheaded with excitement and nervous as hell. She sure as hell didn't want him to know that though. "I wondered if you were going to mention that."

She felt him shrug. "I've accepted it. No reason to beat around the bush about it."

Her shoulders slumped as disappointment whispered through her. She didn't know what she thought he'd say, but that clearly wasn't it. They didn't know each other, and to expect declarations of undying love would be ridiculous. Still, to say you accepted it — it was so… unromantic. He could at least give a girl some glimmer of hope, couldn't he?

She rolled onto her back, tired of talking to the side of the tent. Her eyes widened, a gasp escaping her lips. His eyes glowed above her.

"Don't freak out on me now, pixie," he chuckled, the sound vibrating against her side, sending chills racing through her.

"I'm not," she squeaked, then cleared her throat. "I'm not freaking out. I was surprised, that's all."

"Uh huh. Why is it you're taking this so well? This isn't normal human behavior."

"The mate thing? I like to keep an open mind and go with the flow," she said lightly. He didn't have a clue how much she was freaking out on the inside. It wasn't every day a woman found out she was mated to a shifter.

"No one is that easygoing," he argued, eyebrow arching up.

She rolled her eyes at his disbelief, "Fine. I've known about shifters all my life. We have some that work at the family store, and Nate works with quite a few when he takes people out on trips in the Grand Canyon. And, like I told you before, my roommate is a fox-shifter. She's told me tons about the shifter lifestyle. It's rather fascinating."

"Stories from other people don't prepare someone fully. Why don't I smell her on you, by the way?"

"I'm told her scent is really muted. It has something to do with not letting her vixen out that much. She's not too into the whole outdoors thing. Plus, all the new stuff I have. I stocked up for this trip at my parents' store. Why are your eyes so glowy?" She reached up and touched the side of his face. He leaned in slightly. Stubble scratched at the palm of her hand as she slid it into his hair, the soft, silky strands tickling her fingers. It was exactly as she imagined.

"Because I'm in a tight sleeping bag, lying naked next to my unclaimed mate." His voice dropped low, rumbling from his chest. Thrusting his hips lightly against her side, he let her feel his arousal...not that she wasn't aware of it beforehand.

"You think I'm that easy?" she smirked. Taunting him when she probably shouldn't.

"You did say you liked to go with the flow. I know you're attracted to me."

"And you said no one was that easygoing. Have you changed your mind?"

"No, but you didn't run screaming from the tent when I said you were my mate. If anything, your arousal peaked." He inhaled loudly. "Damn, it smells good too. Light, sweet musk mixed with a hint of roses. My wolf loves it."

"Oh!" On reflex, she pressed her thighs tighter together.

Gideon slid his hand up her torso until he had hold of her breast. He brushed his thumb over the rising bud as he spoke. "I know this is fast, Ryder, and you say you know about shifters, and clearly have some type of understanding of mates; but, do you really know what it all means?"

Ryder swallowed hard and nodded in the darkness. In all of her wolf studies and research, she knew there was a chance he could see her face. "Mates mean I'm destined to be yours. There is a chemical attraction that tells your wolf I belong to you."

"It isn't just chemical, pixie," he rumbled, and pressed his lips against hers. The quick, soft caress ignited a flame within her. Whispered words floated in the back of her mind, but they were too soft for her to make out. She felt his warm breath against her lips, as he lifted his head marginally. "Our wolves are one part of a whole. In order to achieve full unity, they must find the other half of their soul. They recognize it by smell and touch. My wolf was drawn to your scent originally, and when he stuck his snout against your very human neck, he recognized you as his mate. His other half. He wants nothing more than to claim you by bite, tethering you to him for the rest of his life."

"Oh my!" A million butterflies took off in her stomach at the thought. Gideon was offering her the one thing she'd dreamed of her entire life. To be part of the wolf community and all it entailed. *To be part of a pack.* There was only one thing that held her back from her telling him to claim away. "What about you, the man? Is that what you want, or are you only going along because of your wolf? Will you be happy tethered to me, as you put it, for the rest of *your* life?"

He was silent for so long, she didn't think he would answer and, if he did...she was sure she wasn't going to like it. "I'm attracted to you, but I'm not in love, if that's what you're asking. I don't know you well enough, but maybe someday. I'll claim you as my mate because not doing so would cause me harm in the long run. My wolf would reject my being with anyone but you. Physically. Emotionally. There would be a complete breakdown between man and wolf. As Alpha of the Keystone Predators, I would have to give up my position. Become a lone wolf or drop to the lowest level in the Pack. I refuse to do either. I'm a damn good Alpha, and my pack-mates would reject even the slightest suggestion."

Yep, she was right. She didn't like his answer, but she appreciated the honesty. Pretty words and empty promises had never done it for her. "What if I refuse you? What happens then?"

"I would pursue you relentlessly until you caved in. It wouldn't take long. I'm very good at getting what I want." She heard the grin in his voice. She just bet he got what he wanted, when he wanted, no questions asked. As lovely as that all sounded, she wouldn't be rolling over anytime soon. Pretty words may not sway her, but they were necessary at some point.

"You're cocky for a guy that needs my acceptance

of what you're offering. Claiming with a possible, non-guaranteed, chance of love at some point in the future."

Gideon sighed and slipped his hand down to her waist. "I'll give you time if that's what you need, but in return, I need you to make the effort. Agree to move to the compound with me. We have plenty of space, and it would make it easier on us both."

"Move to your compound? That's kind of serious, isn't it?"

"It is, but so is finding your destined mate. Kind of a big deal where I'm from."

Before she had a chance to answer, footsteps could be heard approaching. She jackknifed up. "Oh, my god," she whispered. "Someone's out there."

Gideon pulled her back, forcing her to lie down. "It's my Beta. Give me a minute."

He got out of the sleeping bag. When she heard the zipper on the tent, she snagged her flashlight and shined it at the opening. Kneeling, Gideon looked back at her with his brows furrowed. "You can turn that off. I can see just fine."

"Yeah, but I can't and you're naked," she said, her eyebrows rising into her hairline. A thick-muscled back and broad shoulders faced her. As she let her gaze travel down his body, she felt heat lick against her face. He had the firmest ass she'd had the pleasure of seeing up close. Her fingers itched to pinch it to see if it was really as taut as it looked.

A shock of jet-black hair entered the tent, followed by intense dark eyes. A deeply tanned face stared back at her. His head dropped in a nod before he looked at Gideon.

"You guys okay?" The new man looked between them, and when his gaze landed back on Gideon, he grinned. Bright, straight white teeth gleamed in the darkness. "I waited at the trailhead for a while and figured I would come see if you needed help with your Luna and her gear."

Gideon grunted and turned. Ryder watched as some silent conversation went on between the two men. There were nods and snorts. The other man hovered in the opening as Gideon searched for his clothes, putting them on quickly. He gave a cursory look around her tent and started pack things in her bag.

"Stop!" She sat up, ensuring she stayed covered. Both men looked at her, question written on both their faces. "You don't seriously think I'm going to hike out of here at night, do you?"

The men looked at each other and shrugged. "Yeah," they said in unison.

"Um, no. I don't see as well as you two. The trek back up will be sketchy when it's this dark out, headlamp or no headlamp."

Gideon shuffled over on his knees. "It'll be fine, Ryder. We'll help you."

"And who is the other half of this 'we'?"

"I'm your Beta, Diego." His head dipped again, she figured out of respect for who she was intended to be. It made her a bit uncomfortable. She wasn't officially anything at the moment.

"There will be no arguing about this, Ryder. You can't stay out here tonight. Not with your head injury and a bum ankle. You're going to need help getting around."

"Fine."

Gideon grinned and went back to packing her things.

"You stay out here with me." She crossed her arms over her chest and tipped her chin up.

"Ryder," he warned, his dark eyes glittering.

56

She could tell Gideon wouldn't back down on this. Something about his body language told her so. Waiting a few seconds, she sighed loudly. "You aren't doing that right. Hand me my pack." Holding out her hand, she waited. "Now," she demanded, thrusting her hand at him when he didn't turn it over right away. She could be stubborn about things just as easily.

He handed it over, and she dug the clean clothes out he'd stuffed down in the bottom. Looking at the men, she stared expectantly. When they didn't get the hint, she shooed them out. "Go. I need to get dressed."

"I'll help," Gideon said, attempting to snatch up the bundle of clothes.

"Nope. Out. I can dress myself. I've been doing it since I was a kid. Certainly don't need help now."

He frowned and Diego chuckled before disappearing without a word.

"I'll be right outside if you need help," Gideon said, giving one last look at the clothes balled in her hands then back at her.

She rolled her eyes. "Fine, but I won't. Zip it as you leave, please."

She waited until he left before crawling out of the bag. Gingerly, she looked at, poked, and prodded her damaged ankle. It was still swollen, but not as bad as before. The skin was tender to the touch, but it wasn't anything she couldn't handle. She got dressed then gathered everything into piles. Making quick work, she had everything but the tent packed and ready to go. Gideon popped his head in with a look of surprise on his face. He blinked a couple of times, then shook his head. "It figures you would do it on your own."

"If it'll make you feel manly, you can take the tent down. I always hate that part. There's room for it in the top." She handed the bag to him and crawled out of the tent. Before she could stand, he had his hands under her

57

arms, lifting her out. He kept her feet dangling above the ground as he carried her over to a nearby rock.

"Sit. Stay."

"I'm not a dog. I believe you hold that honor."

He released an irritated sigh, and Diego chuckled.

"I want to check your ankle. Diego, will tear down the tent for us?"

She frowned when he didn't rise to the bait, but didn't object when he unlaced her left boot and pulled her sock off. Picking her battles was her best bet, and this one wasn't worth the fight. "It doesn't feel that bad. I should be able to walk. It'll just take me a little longer."

"I'll carry you," he grunted, while putting the sock and boot back on her.

"You will do no such thing." Pride and outrage warred in her. She went to stand, and he pushed her back down.

"It's my fault you got hurt, and it's my responsibility, my duty, to make sure it doesn't happen again."

"Cool, I love macho bullshit," she said, letting as much sarcasm drip from the words as she could. "Listen, buster." She poked him in the chest to make sure she had his attention. "I don't put up with it from my brothers, and I won't put up with it from you. Mate or not, that shit don't fly."

"You *are* my mate and you *won't* be walking on the ankle."

"*Unclaimed* mate." She shot up and put weight on her foot. She grinned and almost let out a whoop when her knees buckled. She'd forgotten about her other injury. Blood rushed from her head, and her vision went dark. *Shit!*

"Damn it!" Gideon scooped Ryder up before she crumpled to the ground. His heart just about beat out of his chest when her face had gone pale and she'd started to go down.

"She's a feisty one."

"You think," he stated and eyed his Beta, who was trying not to laugh. "You got her pack?"

"Yep. We're ready to hightail it out of here. Shouldn't take long to get back to the trailhead with you carrying her."

"He's not carrying me," Ryder mumbled and squirmed in his arms.

It figured she'd wake up right then. To get her to stop moving, he dropped a heated kiss on her lips, surprised when her little tongue teased along the seam of his lips. He let her in. Allowed her to explore every inch of his mouth she dared to. Her fingers threaded through his hair and tugged, earning a groan from him. The only reason they pulled away from each other was lack of oxygen. He was about to claim her lips again when Diego interrupted.

"I do believe he is, Luna," Diego remarked and walked off whistling.

"Thanks for the reminder, jerk," she called out. "And I'm *not* your Luna. My name is Ryder."

"Whatever you say…Luna." Diego chuckled, slinging her pack onto his shoulder.

Gideon felt her stare land on him, but he didn't look down. If he did, he didn't think he could resist sipping from her lips again. That would lead to him pushing her against the nearest flat surface and burying his cock deep inside her. Which he knew would lead to claiming the pixie whether she agreed to it or not. Adjusting her in his arms, he followed behind Diego.

"Aren't you going to correct him?"

"Nope."

"He's wrong though. I'm not his Luna. You like correcting me when you think I'm wrong, so I figure you like doing it to everyone else."

Gideon snorted and glanced down into her stunning face. Thank fuck for shifter vision. Her eyes glittered, and a blush stole across her cheeks. "Nope."

"Nope to him being wrong or nope, you don't correct everyone but me."

"I told you we're mates."

"Unclaimed mates, so there's still room for things to change."

"I doubt it," he smiled down at her.

The stubborn little pixie pursed her lips tightly and grunted. Seemed she didn't have a comeback for that one.

They made quick work of trekking back to the trailhead. It was one of the perks of being a shifter. Speed and strength carried over to the human side. It would take them a little over two hours to get to their destination because of the terrain.

"Tell me about your family?" He asked just to get her talking again. She'd been silent and fuming for far too long.

"What do you want to know?

"You said you have brothers."

"Three of them. Cameron is the oldest. He's twenty-seven and the biggest stick in the mud out of all of them. He's slowly taking over the store my family owns in Flagstaff; Sparks Sporting and Outdoors. Mom and Dad want to retire in the next couple of years and travel. Cam will do a great job. He's like a damn drill sergeant when the parental units aren't around. Next, there's Nathan. He's twenty-six. Nate runs the tours and excursions for the store, and is at the Grand Canyon most days of the week. He's the biggest outdoor freak of all of us. He can't stand being cooped up in the store. Then, there's my younger brother, Jonathan. Jon's twenty-one and having a super time. He works as little as possible and still plays video games like he's twelve."

Gideon snorted. "What was it like being the only daughter?"

"Equal parts great and horrible. Great because, duh, I'm the only girl. I had my own room and my own bathroom. I didn't have to share any of my things. I mean, they were girl things so, you know, why would they be interested? The flip side was, I was the *only* girl. Cam and Nate were thick as thieves when we were growing up. They never let me play with them, even though I'm not that much younger. I had to wait until Jon came around to have someone to do stuff with, and even he balked when he got older. Things didn't change in high school either. They completely ignored me unless I was interested in a boy. Then they were buddy-buddy with me. Ruining any chances of me dating. I had one year all to myself."

Gideon perked up at that bit of news. The idea of her with another man pissed him off. It also made his wolf want to tear someone's throat out.

"But my family loves me and, as much as they annoy me, I love them."

Gideon didn't fault them in the least, and was happy to hear how her brothers looked out for her. His mate deserved to be protected, even if he hadn't known about her existence. To know her family treated her like the most precious thing in the world made his heart glad. He didn't doubt they would fit in with his world.

The feelings swirling inside him were foreign and, at first, unwelcome. He'd thought to claim her because there was no other option. It was his duty, and Fate dictated it was his time. Now that he knew a little more about her, he wasn't seeing it as much of a duty. Bit by bit he was discovering the task was something he *wanted* to do.

As they crested the last ridge, his gray crew cab truck came into sight. Thank all that was holy; Diego had the presence of mind to bring Gideon's truck and not one of the others. The wolf in him relaxed knowing Ryder would be surrounded by his scent. He didn't want any other scent to overpower his own. The creature wouldn't be satisfied until she was drenched in his scent and marked by his teeth.

Diego hit the button to disarm the alarm and opened the passenger door before moving to the back. Gideon put Ryder in, buckled her up, and jogged around the front to claim the driver's seat.

"My Jeep is at the visitor's center. We can pick it up along the way. I'm sure Diego won't have a problem driving it, unless you don't know stick."

"I'm good with stick," he chuckled from the backseat.

She looked over her shoulder at Diego, a sly little smile playing on her lips. "You trying to tell me something?" She wiggled her eyebrows up and down.

Gideon studied his friend's reflection in the rearview mirror, curious about his response. He'd seen Diego with men and women, but never asked which he'd prefer as a mate.

Diego chuckled good-heartedly, "I don't mind playing both ways. We shifters don't have the hang-ups about sex like you humans do. I'll take my mate from either gender. I know that the Fates will give me the perfect mate."

A look of pleased acceptance glowed from Ryder's face. "That's nice to hear. I hope your mate is everything you hope for." She cocked her head to the side, glancing at Gideon. He saw the challenge on her face. "It's about an hour and a half home. You don't mind do you?"

"Sorry, pixie. Not happening," he said, starting up the truck. They pulled out, and he could feel her eyes on him

62

still.

"What do you mean *not happening*? I'm going to need my Jeep. Since my trip is obviously canceled, you can drive me home and I'll rest up there."

"I told you, you're my mate. Until you've made up your mind and I've claimed you, I can't let you out of my sight."

Her shocked gasp should have been his first clue she wasn't happy about this. The punch in the arm certainly hit that home. "Hey," he said, rubbing the injured spot.

"Oh please, I didn't hit you that hard. You hadn't said anything about that."

"You didn't agree to see me, so I made the decision for you." He peeked at her out of the corner of his eye.

She scowled, her nostrils flaring in anger. It was fucking hot as hell. "That's because happy-go-lucky back there showed up before I could say anything."

"Hey, don't drag me into this, Luna." Gideon snickered.

She turned in her seat to face his friend. "I'm not your Luna, Diego, so stop with that. And for the record, you dragged your ass in it when you showed up uninvited." She flipped him the bird, then turned back to the front, crossing her arms over her chest.

Diego had the good sense to keep his mouth shut. Gideon tapped into his friend's mind while Ryder pouted.

Find her keys. We'll pick up the Jeep, but we're heading back to the compound. I'll deal with her wrath there.

Diego snorted, which earned him a glare from Ryder. *That's all you, man. I like her though.*

A growl rumbled free. Ryder looked at him, rolled her eyes, and went back to staring out the side window.

Not like that, Alpha. Never like that. You need a firm hand next to you, and she won't take shit from anyone, even you. It's the perfect match. I'm surprised you haven't claimed her already.

The wolf wants to. I'm coming around to it, but I think she needs something more.

Of course she does. She's a woman.

Great. They pulled into the visitor's center, finding only one other vehicle. "Your Jeep?"

She nodded sharply. "Keys are in the front middle pocket."

They heard Diego dig them out. He hopped out and headed to her Jeep. Climbing in, Gideon waited until the lights came on before driving off.

"You really aren't going to take me home?"

Gideon felt bad, but he couldn't be separated from her. "We *are* going home."

Confusion coated the words. "But I thought you said…"

He cut her off. "Why don't you curl up and get some rest? You can lean back and turn the heated seats on." He was taking her home. *His* home. Where she belonged from here on out.

She huffed out a resigned breath. "Sure. That sounds nice. My head is bothering me a little anyway. A nap will do me good. Wake me up when we hit the edge of town."

"Okay, pixie." He reached out and ran a hand down her arm. She sighed happily, so he picked up her hand and threaded their fingers together. It would help her with the pain. Not as good as the full body pain relief but, hopefully, enough she could get some rest.

"Sweet dreams," he said once she was situated, rotating onto her left side, facing him. It didn't take long for her eyes to flutter shut and breathing to even out

64

CHAPTER EIGHT

March 19 – 0800

Ryder rolled over, not wanting to wake from the dream she was having. There was a soft mattress under her. Cozy, warm covers surrounding her naked body. The squishy yet slightly firm pillow cradling her head. It was a hiker's dream. To feel all of the comforts of home, but know you were sleeping on the hardened ground.

A rustling next to her pulled her from the fog of her dream. There shouldn't have been anyone or anything rustling. *Unless it's a snake!* She hated snakes! Jerking awake, she shot up and out of the bed, coming face to face with a man. One she didn't know. This was becoming a bad habit.

His eyes popped open wide with surprise, and he took a step back. "Hello," he drawled, after he shook free of the shock. Lust fired in his dark eyes as a slow grin curled up the corner of his lips. "Damn baby, you're hot. I have no clue what he did to deserve you." He whistled appreciatively, as his intense gaze raked over her body.

Glancing down, Ryder squealed. She slapped one

65

arm across her breasts and covered her crotch with the other. Damn it! She was naked for real and totally not on the campground at all. Swiveling her head, she frantically searched for something to cover up with, grabbing the first thing that would do the trick. Snatching up a pillow, she thrust it in front of her, hugging it tight. "Who the hell are you?"

"Baby, I'm anybody you want me to be." He wiggled his eyebrows and grinned.

"God, I hope that line doesn't actually work. If so, the woman of the world are dumber than I thought." She wanted to scoot around him, but she didn't know where she'd go. The bank of curtain windows to her right was open and, unless she felt like mooning anyone that might be outside, that wasn't an option. She could crawl back over the bed, but that meant exposing herself that way as well. She eyed the guy in front of her, wondering if she should risk it. There was a good probability she wouldn't be fast enough to escape him.

He was tall, probably about her brother Jon's almost six-foot frame. He had a swimmers build. Corded muscles defined his arms. His thick, broad chest and shoulders stretched the dark grey t-shirt molded to his torso. Well-worn dark jeans hung low on his hips and hugged his muscular legs. For the love of Moses, he didn't have any shoes on. Why was seeing a man's bare feet such a turn-on when they wore jeans? *Why are you staring at his feet?* Her inner voice had a point.

She ripped her stare away and looked at his face. There was something slightly familiar about him. Dark, wavy brown hair. Twinkling brown eyes. His full lips curved into that cock-sure half smile.

She wanted to smack herself on the forehead. If it had been any more obvious, it would have knocked her the hell over.

"Holy shit, Gideon has a brother?"

"That's right, sweet cheeks. A *much* younger brother."

"Obviously," she snorted without thought. He sounded just like *her* younger brother, Jon.

A low, menacing snarl sounded on the other side of the room. Their heads turned in the direction of it, and she saw Gideon — teeth bared, fists clenched, and eyes glowing brightly. He stood in the doorway to the room, a thin mist swirling at his feet. If looks could kill, this kid would be dead.

He took a step forward, and Ryder instinctively stepped back. It was like they were in the creek again, except this time his gaze was zeroed in on the guy in front of her. She bumped into the side table knocking over a glass of water. The guy she assumed was Gideon's brother, casually moved away from her.

"Calm down, bro. I only came in to drop off the pain meds and water like you asked. If it was *that* big of a deal, you should have done it." He inched closer to the windows, slowly stripping out of his clothes. Reaching behind him, he yanked his t-shirt off over his head and dropped it to the floor. "Hey sweet cheeks, press that blue button on the remote for me. It's on the table behind you." When his hands went to the button of his jeans, she looked away and reached for the remote. Smashing the blue button, the windows that weren't normal windows started to slide open, revealing a four-foot ledge then wide-open territory.

"Nice to meet you, Luna," he chuckled, grabbing her attention again. She watched in pure fascination as he dove out the window, shifting from human to wolf. It was magnificent. Dropping her pillow, she dashed to the open space, looking to see where he went. A dark brown wolf loped off across the lawn to a field further behind. He'd just gone out of sight when strong arms closed around her waist and plucked her up off the floor.

*****

"No more," Gideon growled and dropped Ryder on the bed. He followed her down, covering her body with his own. God, it felt like a dream to have her under him. Her soft feminine body pressed against his hard edges. His cock nestled against her core.

His wolf within pushed him to mark, mate, and claim their woman. Spending the entire night wrapped around her had made it damned difficult to resist. The light rose scent she carried enveloped him, filtering into his lungs every time he took a breath. It intoxicated him, made his head swim. He could do nothing but think of her; whether he was awake or dreaming. The feel of her warm skin against his soothed him, opening a place in his heart he didn't know existed. He was done resisting. It was time to figure this shit out and claim his mate.

To soothe the savage beast beating against his chest, he took her mouth in a hard, possessive kiss. Like a trigger in his brain, he saw flashes of their future...nights of running together beneath the silver light of the moon. Evenings spent loving one another in front of the roaring fire. Three sweet little girls with dark curly hair like their mother's, and one serious older boy towering over them protectively. It was his future family.

His heart stopped in his chest momentarily before taking off, galloping out of control. Peace settled around him, in his heart and in his head. His future was mewling beneath him and if his visions were anything to go by, and they usually were, he was in for the time of his life.

"Gideon," she moaned softly, arching against him, scattering the visions.

Now that he'd seen what their future could hold, there was no way he would stop. His plan to take it slow flew out the window. Making his way down her jaw and neck, he licked the fluttering juncture where neck and shoulder met. He nipped it and sucked hard. Marking her in the least invasive way for the time being. He would be back to sink his fangs in as soon as he was buried deep inside her. As soon as he felt her quiver around his dick.

Gideon moved down her body, kissing and nipping

every inch of flesh along the way. Shouldering between her thighs, he slid his hands beneath her ass and lifted. He closed his eyes and breathed in deep, before exhaling on a sigh. "Damn, you smell delicious."

A nervous giggle had him opening his eyes.

"You okay?"

"Oh yeah," she replied a little too brightly. Her hands fluttered in front of her. "But, um, just so you know, I haven't really gotten around to," she waved her hand miming between them, "ya' know — doing it — with a guy."

Gideon blinked rapidly and raised his head. He studied the gorgeous body laid out in front of him, wondering how that could be possible, and then back to study her face. Her cheeks were a beautiful shade of pink. Her lips glossy from repeated swipes of her tongue. Her breath stuttered out unevenly.

"You haven't…" he wanted her to say it. *Needed* to hear directly from her lips what he thought she was trying to say. There wasn't any room for him to make a mistake.

"Had sex," she blurted, then covered her face with her hands.

Gideon crawled back up her body and slid off to the side. Sorry to have to leave the bounty that awaited him, but so much more intrigued by what would happen later. Leaning on his elbow, he peeled her hands from her face, holding them together on her stomach.

"Say that again," he whispered.

She scowled at him before rolling her eyes. Leave it to her to be vulnerable one second and irritated the next. "I am as pure as freshly fallen snow. No one has popped my cherry. I still carry my V-Card. Basically, I haven't found a man I've wanted to give my virginity to."

Gideon held up his hand to stop the flow of words from her. "Got it. You're a virgin." The words came out sounding calm but…*holy shit!* Where did he start with that bit of information? He knew what he wanted to do, but what if she wasn't on board. "So, this is a pretty big deal then?"

"Ya' think?" She looked at him, eyes rounded. "This is a weird conversation to have naked. Especially since we're no longer fooling around."

"Pixie, I wasn't fooling. I planned on making you come with my mouth, and then fucking you senseless and, finally, claiming you." He rolled off the bed to stand. He needed her covered up and less tempting. Scooping her up, he tucked her back under the covers, pulling them up to her chin. "How about you get some more sleep?"

She snorted and tossed the covers off. "Not the most subtle change of topic. How about we finish this conversation and see what happens next?" She got up and looked around slightly confused. "Where's my pack?"

"I put it away. You don't need it."

"If we aren't having sex, I will need clothes." Walking over to his dresser, she started opening and closing the drawers. "Don't you have any t-shirts I can wear?"

Shaking his head in regret, he went to the closet and grabbed her a shirt. While he was in there, he adjusted his dick behind the zipper of his jeans. *Damn, she's a virgin.* The thought of being the first *and* last man to ever touch her, to bring her pleasure and satisfaction…it scared the shit out of him almost as much as it made his dick hard, and that thing was rock-fucking-hard. Pound-nail-and-not-even-notice hard.

He sucked in a calming breath and walked out. He found Ryder perched in the middle of his bed, comforter wrapped around her tightly, as she craned her neck to look out the still open wall of windows. What happened in the two minutes he'd been in the damn closet?

"There's a bunch of people out there, pretending they aren't looking up here. They totally are, and I think they

70

saw my ass."

Gideon looked out and, sure enough; a good chunk of the Pack was milling about the lawn that led into the field behind their home. They tried for casual, but he knew they were being nosy. Word must have gotten out about Ryder being their Luna. Shit, that meant his parents would be showing up soon. He'd deal with that later. First, he needed to figure out what was going on with his mate, and what his next move was.

He headed back to the table by the bed that held the curtain window remote, and hit the button to close up the windows. Next, he tapped the one that would trigger the auto frost. There were times, like now, when he wanted privacy. Most of the time he kept them open. He liked to smell the fresh air and feel the sunlight beaming down.

He handed the t-shirt to Ryder, who slipped it on over her head. She crawled to the head of the bed and leaned against the headboard, patting the spot next to her in invitation.

Gideon eyed the bed warily. Not sure he could stand sitting next to her, especially knowing she had nothing on under his shirt. Shit, he didn't think he could actually take sitting next to her period. Not without dragging her down onto the mattress and claiming her.

"I won't bite," she joked.

"I might," he mumbled, sitting down, keeping an arm's length between them, which she proceeded to completely ignore.

She shimmied over and forced her way under his arm. "I'm a virgin, not a communicable disease."

An awkward silence descended upon them. He didn't have the slightest clue what to say. The last time he'd been with a virgin, he'd been one too, and that was like a lifetime ago.

"So…" he said, but had nothing to follow it up with.

71

Ryder laughed. "I didn't know it was such a big deal. I was nervous and giggled. When you looked at me, I felt I should let you know. I didn't mean for you to stop."

"What did you think I would do? I'm not an asshole who wouldn't care."

"Take it slow," she said with uncertainty.

He grunted and stroked a hand down her arm. "I'm not sure what to do now. There's a ton we don't know about each other, but the longer I'm around you; the more I want you. And, the more I'm driven to claim you."

"I know the wolf does but..." He pressed a finger to her lips. Their softness dipping under the pressure.

"Me. The wolf wants you just fine and as much, if not more, than before. He thinks I'm taking way too long with this."

"I'll say," she said under her breath, but he heard her just fine.

"Am I the guy you want to give your virginity to?"

Ryder turned to face him. "Yes. We're mates. What better person to take my virginity than the man I'm destined to be with for the rest of my life?"

Gideon's lips thinned in irritation. "Do you really believe that?" He didn't know why her answer ticked him off. He had all but told her the only reason he was with her was because they were mates, and it would hurt him to be without her. He couldn't expect more from her if he wasn't willing to give the same. He just didn't know if he was there yet. Sure, he acknowledged they were mates, and he didn't plan on resisting the pull. To give his heart away though — that was a different matter.

She must have seen the turmoil on his face. Climbing onto his lap, she smoothed her thumb over his brow. "Gideon. I like you regardless of how much you like to tell me I'm wrong. I'm seriously attracted to you. You've got a smokin' hot body I want to climb like a damn monkey."

He smirked, and she pressed a kiss to his lips. Short but sweet, just like his pixie.

"We're mates and I know what that means for shifters. I know the torture you'll go through, according to my roommate Pansy, if you don't claim me. I'm willing to let you do that. I'm willing to take what you can give me now. I'll warn you though, I hope to fall in love with you one day, and I pray you'll do the same."

He could have told her they would be in love with one another. He'd seen it in his vision. He held back. He wanted her feelings for him to come without persuasion. He nodded slightly, agreeing to all she said.

She grasped his face with both hands. The warmth and feel of them slid beneath his skin. His wolf stretched and nudged from inside. He knew his eyes were beginning to glow. She searched his face, looking for lord knew what, then grinned. "Claim me, Gideon," she whispered and kissed him tenderly. The touch of her lips against his was a drug traveling through his veins. Heavy and sweet, it pulsed and pushed past all of the barriers leading to his heart. Like a sweet addiction, he couldn't get enough.

Tumbling her onto her back, he stayed to the side. Trailing a hand down the middle of her chest, he made a beeline for her sweet pussy. Working his fingers into the delicate folds, she gasped and arched up. The perfume of her arousal swelled around them, and just when he starting inching down, the loud clearing of someone's throat pulled him from his Ryder-induced daze. Eyes narrowed and ready to blast the person who dared interrupt, Gideon did a double take when he saw his mom standing in the doorway, arms crossed over her chest, foot tapping a rapid tattoo on the floor.

"Fuck," he groaned and dropped his head onto Ryder's stomach.

"Not right now you aren't. Get up off your mate right this minute, Gideon Maxwell Deckard. I can't believe you didn't tell us immediately."

Ryder pushed against his head. "Gideon, move" she whispered harshly. Panic and embarrassment threaded through her voice. Her body was strung tight beneath him, all remnants of arousal gone.

He groaned and started to stand. Grabbing the hem of her shirt, he pulled it down tightly over her body. His dad took that moment to step up behind his mom. "Let's go, son. We want to meet your new mate."

"I'll be right there, sir." Filled with resignation, he helped Ryder up. Pulling her into the closet with him, he found her backpack stuffed in a corner. Rummaging through, he found a tiny pair of panties and handed them to her.

She took them and wiggled into them. "Where are the clothes I had on last night?"

He pulled them from a shelf, handing them over reluctantly. He was so close to getting a taste of her.

After getting dressed, they took a couple minutes in the bathroom to clean up. She came out looking less tousled. His wolf whimpered at the loss.

She clapped her hands together, a determined look on her face. "Okay, let's do this."

"You're a little too excited about this I think."

"Nope, but if we keep getting interrupted, I'll be a virgin forever. Neither of us wants that."

Gideon snorted and placed a hand at the small of her back. He guided her down the stairs, steering her toward the kitchen. "You're one of a kind, Ryder." He bent, kissing her on the top of her head.

She smirked and turned into him. She got up on tiptoes, flung her arms around his neck, and pulled him down for a sultry, devouring of his lips. "Don't you forget it," she said huskily.

74

CHAPTER NINE

March 19 – 10:00am

Ryder steeled herself and walked into the kitchen with her head held high. Gideon's brother sat on a barstool, head hanging low like he'd gotten in trouble. He probably had. He peeked at her from beneath his lashes and mouthed *sorry*.

She shrugged as if it were no big deal and made her way to the coffeemaker. It was one of those one-cup-at-a-time brewers like they had at the store. A stack of cups sat to the right and a carousal of little coffee brewing packs to the left. Spinning it, she picked one that looked familiar, snatched up a mug, and brewed a cup.

She turned and leaned against the counter as she waited for it to finish.

The man and woman, who she assumed were Gideon's parents, sat at the kitchen dinette, each with a mug in front of them. They watched her with frank curiosity while the boys sulked.

Gideon went to his mother's side and kissed her on

the cheek before coming to stand next to Ryder. Tension in the room built, as no one said anything. His parents sat there expectantly, while Gideon puttered around the kitchen, acting as if his parents hadn't just interrupted them in his room. The coffeemaker sputtered, so she turned back to it and took out her mug. Gideon opened the top and took the used brew cup out, throwing it away for her.

"There's creamer in the fridge and sugar in the canister over there."

"I'm good." Taking her mug, she went to the dinette. It appeared she'd have to be the one to wear the big girl panties. Setting the cup down, she held her hand out to Gideon's mom. "I'm Ryder Sparks. From what Gideon tells me, we're mates."

The woman's dark eyebrows raised a fraction before a grin lifted the corners of her mouth. "It's nice to meet you dear. I'm Florence Deckard and this is my husband, Stephen."

Ryder nodded to the older version of Gideon. She sat down and waited to see what would happen next. They all turned their heads to look at Gideon.

Lips pinched tight, he joined them at the table. "Might as well sit with us, Forrest," he grumbled.

"You two are acting like you're going to the executioner," Ryder commented, looking between Gideon and Forrest as they sat down.

Forrest snorted, earning him a glare from his mother. "Sorry," he mumbled and hung his head.

Gideon slid his hand onto her thigh and squeezed lightly. "Mom, Dad, I've found my mate."

Stephen rolled his eyes at his son. "We gathered that, son. When did you meet her? Why did we have to hear through Pack gossip that you'd found her?" He squinted his eyes and stared at Ryder's neck. "Why haven't you claimed her yet?"

Ryder's hand automatically went to her neck. The warmth of the hickey heated her palm, and she flushed in embarrassment.

"No need to cover that up dear. Stephen used to give them to me all of the time." Florence giggled. "Still does sometimes," she wiggled her eyebrows, and Ryder was reminded of Forrest.

Both boys groaned in disgust.

"Mom," Forrest whined. "We don't want to know stuff like that."

"Oh, pooh!" She waved her hand and winked at Ryder.

"My parents are the same way. I'm used to that kind of thing," Ryder said to ease the tension.

Florence's eyes lit up with pleasure. "Tell me about your family, dear."

"Wait," Stephen interrupted. "Let's get some answers from our son first. Gideon?"

"I met Ryder yesterday morning out on the Grandview Trail."

"Oh?" Florence leaned close to Ryder and sniffed. "But you aren't a shifter."

Ryder smiled. "No ma'am. I'm strictly human. I was on a four-day trek when I ran into your son."

"More like tripped and fell," Gideon mumbled next to her.

Ryder turned and childishly stuck her tongue out at him. "It was your fault I fell. You shouldn't have started toward me."

Gideon's eyebrows rose. "You shouldn't have tried

getting closer to me. I'm a wild animal."

"So you keep saying," she snorted, then slapped her hand over her mouth.

Forrest snickered, earning a slap on the back of his head from his dad.

"You must have some wolf in your bloodline somewhere, dear, otherwise you wouldn't be Gideon's mate." Florence leaned forward on her elbows and looked excitedly between them. "So you met, then what? I need every detail so I can tell it to my friends."

Ryder sat up straighter. *Tell it to her friends? All of it!* Hell, no.

Gideon let out an aggrieved sigh. His mother wouldn't back down until she knew everything. He knew that and from the horrified look on Ryder's face, she wouldn't be getting the answers from her. It was funny how a person regressed when their parents were around. It'd been a dick move to not introduce Ryder to them. He was still fuming from being interrupted. He should be balls deep in his mate, and with her screaming the house down.

He shored up his nerves. "I rescued her from the freezing creek bed. She hit her head pretty hard and twisted her ankle. Diego came to get us last night, and we got back to the compound sometime around midnight. I haven't had time to tell you. Ryder only got up a little bit ago."

Ryder snorted. "Don't try to blame my sleeping in for you not calling your parents."

His mom leaned back in her seat and picked up her coffee. "You could have called right when you got home last night, or this morning before she got up. I know you, Gideon. You get up at the crack of dawn no matter what time you go to bed. I hate that Meredith knew before me. Damn busybody," she grumbled.

Forrest leaned around Gideon and pinned Ryder with a mischievous grin. The hackles on the back of Gideon's neck rose. It didn't matter that it was his brother. She was unclaimed, and his wolf was possessive of her.

"Meredith is mom's best friend. They are forever trying to one up each other. The fact that Meredith knew before mom is major."

Gideon studied Ryder as she listened at Forrest. How pissed would she be if he marked her right where they were sitting? It'd make him feel a hell of a lot better. Calm his wolf enough that Ryder could be around others.

Gideon nixed the idea for now. His mom stared at him, eyebrow cocked up, lips compressed. What was it she'd been on about? Oh yeah. "You're right, Mom. I should have let you know when I knew," Gideon said indulgently, ignoring Forrest's snickering. "My mind was preoccupied with other things. Ryder was hurt and she's my first priority."

Apparently satisfied with his answer, his mom stood up. "Good." She moved into the kitchen and started pulling things out of the fridge. Typical behavior for her. The house was as much theirs as it was his. "We should call your parents and have them come out for breakfast. Do you live far, Ryder?"

"In Flagstaff."

"*With* your parents?" His mom pressed.

Ryder took a drink of her coffee. At least he'd learned one thing about her. She liked her coffee strong and black. "No ma'am. I share an apartment with a friend."

Gideon's mom stopped what she was doing and looked at Ryder. "How old are you?"

"I'm twenty-four."

"Jesus," Gideon whispered. He was robbing the damn cradle.

"What was that for?" She turned affronted eyes on him. "How old are you?"

"Almost thirty." He scrubbed a hand over his face. He was learning to shift by the time she was born. Five fucking years! Forrest was closer in age to her than he was. "Damn, I'm old."

"You didn't seem to care earlier."

"That was before I knew how young you were," he raged.

"It's only five years, Gideon. At least I'm not some bubbly eighteen-year-old barely out of high school. Would it make you feel better if I count your grey hairs? There aren't *that* many."

"No, it would *not* make me feel better," he grunted and stood, if only so she couldn't do what she'd said. He knew he was old.

Ryder's unladylike snort almost had him smiling. "Good thing I'm into grumpy older guys." She got up from her chair and kissed him, pulling away much to soon in his opinion.

He cleared his throat when he heard chuckling coming from his dad and brother. "Mom's right. We should invite your parents out."

"Fantastic idea, except for a couple things. One, I'm supposed to be on a four-day trek. There's one more day left before they expect to hear from me. Any contact before then would be like calling out the National Guard. They would imagine the worst and hope for the best."

"I'm sure they won't mind hearing from you before your deadline," Gideon said.

She narrowed her eyes at him, fire spitting from their green depths. "Did you not just hear what I said? You want them to have heart attacks, don't you? It would be easier for you if they were dead. Then you wouldn't have to worry about taking their only daughter away from them and turning her into a wolf."

"Uh…" Gideon looked at his family, then back at her. "No?"

"Dork, of course not. The other issue is they've been at work for about two hours already. Thursdays and Fridays are fairly busy. Everyone tends to get ready for his or her weekend trips on those days."

"How about Saturday? Is there anyone to cover for them at the store?"

"They work the odd weekends now and then. If I remember correctly, they're off this weekend. They wanted to spend the weekend with me after my trip. I'm sure dad wants a debriefing about the gear I took too."

"That's settled then," Stephen announced. "We'll have your parents out on Saturday. They can stay the weekend too. I'm hoping by then my son will have done the right thing."

*****

The right thing? What the hell did that even mean? She sure as shit wouldn't be agreeing to marry him before the weekend was out. As cool as she was about being his mate, she wasn't too sure she loved him. Not yet. They needed more time together. He had to feel the same way. Didn't he?

Ryder looked to Gideon, who blatantly ignored her. Gideon, his father, and his brother went into the kitchen to help out, leaving her wondering what the cryptic message meant. She wouldn't get the answers standing there twiddling her thumbs. Her best tactic would be to insert herself into the mix. Try to become part of the family.

As she rinsed out her coffee cup, Gideon came up behind her, placing his hands on her hips. The rest of the world fell away as the warmth from his chest seeped into her back. A musk that was all him and all male swirled

81

around her, pulling her into a fog. Her breath caught in her throat and her tummy fluttered when he placed his lips next to her ear. "We'll talk later, okay?"

She nodded. They would talk. She'd make sure of it.

CHAPTER TEN

March 19 – 4:00pm

"What do you mean you invited the Pack?" Gideon stared down at his dad, wondering what fresh hell this was. Last he'd checked; he was the fucking Alpha. Not his father! Not anymore.

"You know they expect it. You've kept them from the house the entire day. A place they've always had the freedom to roam. They know you have your Luna here, and they want to meet her."

"Yes, my *unclaimed* Luna," he stated harshly. It was killing him that he'd yet to get ten minutes alone with her since his parents' arrival. And, if it wasn't his parents, it was his brother monopolizing her time.

She should have been focused on him, not them. But then, as a human, she wouldn't feel that powerful tug until he'd marked her for the first time. After that, it would be a slow burning craving sliding through her veins. Five bites in total. That's how many it would take before she would be completely, irrevocably bound to him. He'd yet to sink his teeth into her even once. And now his father expected him to let her near other wolves. Other men who would want to get close to her.

Gideon rolled his shoulders. His muscles bunched and burned with the force of his wolf. The creature wouldn't stand for it. *He* wouldn't stand for it.

An ache formed in the front of his head. It was rare for a shifter to suffer from trivial things like headaches, but this was all too much.

"It isn't my fault you haven't claimed her," his father quipped.

"Yes, it is," he said, throwing his hands up in the air. His father had asked for a couple of minutes alone with him. If he'd known what the conversation was going to be about, he would have refused. But as his sire, Gideon granted his wish. Though his father wasn't Alpha anymore, he still commanded respect. "I was this close to claiming her this morning when we were rudely interrupted."

His father kicked back in Gideon's office chair, plopping his bare feet on the desk. "You should have locked the door."

Gideon knew it was useless to argue with the man. He was still cowed by his father at the age of twenty-nine.

Rubbing the bridge of his nose with finger and thumb, Gideon gave in. "What time are they expected?"

His father grinned and looked at the large clock on the wall. "You've got an hour." Dropping his feet from the desk, he stood and strolled to the closed door. "I suggest you make your first mark. They'll expect to see it, and it'll solidify her position."

Opening the door, they were surprised to see Ryder, hand raised in the air to knock. She dropped it and looked worriedly from father to son.

Gideon's dad looked at him over his shoulder. "She's

a strong one." He let Ryder into the room, then left, closing the door behind him.

"What's wrong?" She asked, crossing the room to join him by the bookcase. She went into his arms easily, hands cupping the sides of his face. He felt instant relief from the pounding in his head. He could only imagine how strong their connection would be once she was marked.

"My parents have invited the Pack over for the evening. They'll be here in an hour," he sighed, reveling in the feel of her warm hands on him.

"I thought you were the Alpha."

"I am, but my father was before me."

"When did you take over?" She turned him and steered him toward the desk. Forcing him to sit on the edge, she situated herself between his legs. The corner of his mouth curved as she swept her hands over his shoulders, kneading the tense muscles. She was taking care of him. Soothing him.

He shut his eyes and just enjoyed it. "Four years ago. Pack members will always give him the respect he deserves. The same they'll do for us when our son takes over."

Soft lips pressed against his, filling him with joy. He looped his arms around her waist and pulled her in tight.

"Our son," she murmured between kisses.

This probably wasn't the best way to have this conversation, but fuck it. He'd roll with it. "One day," he replied. His visions didn't tell him when, only that it would happen. He feathered kisses along her jaw and down her neck.

She hummed appreciatively. "That'll be nice. I have brothers. I'll know what to do." Her words were breathless and sweet music to his ears. She wiggled closer when he buried his face in the crook of her neck. Licking the sensitive skin between neck and shoulder.

"Ryder," he said, lips grazing her soft skin.

"Yes, Gideon."

"I'm going to mark you." Letting his fangs drop, he scraped the area he was about to bite.

She pressed into him, tilting her head to the side. "About time," she said.

His teeth pierced her skin, sliding beneath the surface. Her sweet, tangy blood coated his tongue as he swallowed it down. A barely there mist formed around them, Gideon's wolf calling to the wolf spirit locked away inside Ryder.

Ryder moaned, sliding her hands into his hair, fisting his locks. Shifting his hands to her ass, he lifted her, urging her to spread her thighs around his waist. She dry humped him. Rolling her covered pussy along the ridge of his cock. He helped her along, knowing she would need to orgasm before he could let go.

The mist around them grew thicker. Heavier. His heart raced out of control. He felt the moment the wolves met. A slam to his psyche, a tentative thread connecting him to his mate. The echo of two wolves calling each other sounded in the room. Ryder gasped. Her body going rigid, she called out his name. Gideon couldn't do anything but follow her under. The tight clasp of her thighs. The heat of her core pushing through the layers of clothes. He rocked his hips, coming in his jeans like an untried teen.

Only when her body slumped against him did he pull his teeth free. He licked the wound, speeding the healing process. If all of their markings were as powerful as this one, he would die a happy man.

CHAPTER ELEVEN

March 19 – 10:00pm

Gideon was done sharing his mate. The Pack members arrived promptly at five and the closest he'd gotten to Ryder all evening was when they opened the door together. He had yet to get another moment alone with her and he was completely fed up. He could see the exhaustion on her face, even though she tried to mask it, as she talked with two women.

He'd been surprised and pleased how easily she fit in with everyone. Not a single soul was unhappy with their Luna-to-be. After taking over four years ago, they were thrilled to see their Alpha settling down and he had gotten nothing but glowing adulations on what a wonderful, thoughtful woman she was.

The two women stood and bowed to Ryder. She stood and hugged them each, causing both women to blush fiercely. Gideon took that as his cue to swoop in and steal her away.

"My Luna," He said, offering his arm. She clutched him like he was her lifeline, leaning into his body. She sighed in relief and he looked down, noticing she was in more pain than she'd let him see.

Pain etched the corners of her eyes. Her lips pinched together tightly. "Why didn't you say you needed to lay down? Your ankle and head are still bothering you, aren't they?"

She nodded and limped slightly.

Frustrated in her attempt to keep a brave face, he swept her up in his arms and stormed from the room. Bolting up the stairs, he slammed his bedroom door shut, locked it, undressed her and tucked her into bed. Stripping, he followed suit, pulling her into the curve of his body. He kept his arm loose around her waist, not wanting to crush her completely.

"Thank you," she whispered, and wiggled her ass against him.

"Stop, Ryder. You're exhausted."

"I'm not *that* exhausted. I feel a ton better now that you're here with me. Almost, no pain at all."

"Uh huh."

"I thought once you'd marked me, I would heal up?"

Gideon rolled his eyes at that bit of misinformation. "Who told you that?"

"Forrest."

"Figures."

Ryder rolled in his arms and stroked his face. "I take it your brother was wrong."

"It's a bit more complicated than one bite. You need rest, not a long drawn out conversation."

She stuck her lower lip out in a pout. All he wanted to do was nip it and suck it into his mouth. If he did, he didn't think he'd be able to stop. First her lip, then her neck again. He'd leave a trail of kisses down across her chest. Sucking her cherry nipples in turn. He pushed that direction of his thoughts from his brain. It wasn't what she needed at the moment. The woman didn't have a clue how she tempted him, how she pushed his control.

"I can rest later. I want to spend time with you like I did with everyone else tonight. You don't know how many times I've been asked when were we going to have kids. Did I know what I was getting into? Have I met the ex-girlfriend that you recently broke up with? A few people were surprised she wasn't your Luna, but the majority is glad she isn't. What's up with that? Were you dating some power-hungry bitch?"

Gideon couldn't stop his chuckle. His ex *had been* a power-hungry bitch in every way. "You might say that."

"You'll be happy to know I don't have a boyfriend, by the way." She smoothed her hands down his chest, and one wrapped around his side. Her fingers lightly danced up his back before scraping down ever so lightly. Tingles ran down his spine, landing in his balls. His cock filled and he was forced to ignore the reaction.

"Good," he growled, not liking the thought of any man other than him in her life. *Possessive there, buddy?* Yeah. He was. "I didn't expect to find my mate." He didn't know why the words tumbled from his mouth. Maybe it was so she'd know he wasn't hoping from bed to bed looking for *the* one. Maybe it was because he was finding their connection and her presence stronger than he'd thought it would be at first.

"I doubt anyone does," she replied smartly.

"After my breakup, I wanted to go wolf for a week and sow some wild oats."

She pushed back from him, but didn't break free of his hold on her. "Don't you think you're a little old to be doing that? Not the going wolf part. The sowing your oats part."

"It doesn't matter now. I have you. I have my mate."

She crinkled that button nose and kissed him. "Yes, or at least a mate in the making."

There was something Gideon needed to know. He'd bitten her once. If she wanted to be free of him, she could still leave. They weren't completely tethered together yet. "You aren't going to wake up one day wondering what the hell you did, are you? You're so damn young, pixie."

"You're worse than a girl," she frowned.

"Excuse me?"

"I told you I wanted what you had to offer. I won't change my mind. There is something about you, you big dummy that pulls me in like a tractor beam. There is no escape and I don't want one. We've known each other only a couple days, but I don't care. I want you. End of story. We'll figure the rest out as we go."

Gideon pulled her closer to his body, anchoring her in place with his arms. "Do you know how it's done?"

"Sex or claiming? I've watched porn. I have sex toys, and I'm not afraid to use them. Just because I haven't had sex with a man, and definitely no women…before you ask, it doesn't mean I'm clueless about what goes on."

Damn, that image blew his mind. He'd love to watch her play with herself. To see her slide a dildo into her hot cunt, getting off before he took her. He would have to leave that fantasy for later and once he got a look at her toys. "Claiming," he ground out.

"Oh, that. Based on this afternoon, I have a slight idea. First, you'd lick the spot right there." Wiggling closer, he felt her tongue glide over the pulse point in his neck. There was no stilling the shudder that overtook him.

"Then you'd sink those long, hard teeth into me again." Tiny human teeth grazed his neck, making him

90

shudder. She nipped him and he bucked. His already hard cock jumped, brushing against the soft skin of her belly.

"Ryder," he warned her through clenched teeth.

"Come on, Gideon," she purred. "I want you to take me. Claim me and make me yours." Light kisses rained down on his neck and up over his jaw, before nipping him on the chin. "I want everything you have to offer. I told you that and I meant every word." Her hand trailed down his face and neck; traveled over his chest then around to his ass. With a firm grip she tugged him, trying to pull him forward. There was nowhere else to go. They were glued together from chest to toes. When she wasn't able to get closer, she played dirty. Her leg came up, hooking over his hip. She tilted her pelvis until the soft petal lips of her pussy encased his erection.

One slow roll up and down and he snapped. Gideon couldn't take it any more. He rolled her onto her back, wedging himself between her thighs. Her legs instantly wrapping around his hips. "You're being a tease, Ryder."

"No," she said, looping her arms around his neck. "I'm trying to get what I want."

He chuckled and kissed her quickly. "What is that, pixie?" His voice was low and gruff.

She rolled her hips again and they both moaned. "Your cock inside me."

"Don't you want me to take it slow?" he forced out. He desperately wanted to shove his dick in her, feel her heat caress his length.

"No. I'm over slow and easy, Gideon. We can try that later. However many times you need. I want you and, if I'm honest, I'm afraid someone is gong to bust open your door and stop us again. I don't want you to stop. Not until you make me yours."

His chuckle was strained, but he understood what she was saying. "Four more times, pixie." Reaching down, he moved his cock into position. "I need to mark you four more times, and my cock *will* be in you each time." Her entrance clenched, laying a heated kiss on the head. With as much restraint as he could muster, he slowly worked his way inside.

Small fingernails dug into his shoulders, and he focused on the slight pain to keep himself in check. In and out he pumped his hips. Going deeper with each thrust.

Ryder gasped. Little sounds of delight escaping her lips. "Oh God, Gideon. Please," she begged. "I need you."

"God, yes," he ground out. "Stay with me, pixie. I'm going to make you fly." His fangs descended. He licked the spot on her neck and prepared her for his bite.

The friction of her clasping tight pussy kept him from fully retreating. Her slim legs wrapped around his waist, heels digging into his ass. It was too much. Slamming his hips forward, he sunk his teeth into her neck simultaneously. Fresh, darkly sweet blood rushed into his mouth. His wolf howled in approval. He felt Ryder's wolf drift on the mist again, twining with his, locking him in place.

Ryder screamed his name as she came around his cock, breaking the lock on his body. Her eyes popped open, a dim glow emanated from the depths. Her wolf's soul tangling with her very human one. With a feral growl, he gave up all pretenses, thrusting in and out of her sweet, supple body. The acceptance of him and his wolf drove him to a quick completion. He came inside her, his semen erupting in a hot tidal wave, her name dripping from his lips. He collapsed on top of her, reluctantly shifting to the side. Gathering her in his arms, he curled around her, protecting her, and together they fell asleep.

CHAPTER TWELVE

March 20 – 8:00am

Ryder couldn't sleep any longer. Every ache and pain previously thrumming through her body was practically gone. A renewed energy spiked her bloodstream, making her want to get up and run a damn marathon. Not that that would happen, though. She had something much better in mind. *Like playing with my mate.*

Rolling onto her side, she studied the man slumbering on his back next to her. An arm was draped over his eyes, shutting the world out. The covers were pushed down to his waist, showing off his chiseled, furry chest. The dark hair begging her to run her fingers through it. *Yummy!* Ever so carefully, so as not to wake him, she tiptoed her fingers over his skin, down until she reached the edge of the sheet. *To lift or not to lift? That is the question.* Running one finger lightly along the edge, she debated what she wanted to do next.

After taking her virginity the night before, Gideon curled his body around hers and didn't let go. Sometime during the night they roused, his hard cock poking her from behind. She lifted her leg and curled it back over his hip. He took her hard and fast. Sliding his dick in from behind. Strumming her clit with one hand while the other held onto her breast. When she came, he sunk his teeth into her again, and that sweet blissful edge of pain rode her into another orgasm, one that pulled him with her.

She had yet to have the chance to explore his body. To touch all of the places that intrigued her. A scar that wrapped around one hip. A puckered area in his shoulder that looked like a healed bullet wound. The raised area on his back that she'd yet to lay eyes on. She still hadn't licked and nipped each and every inch of his skin. Nor had she sucked his thick cock between her lips. She wanted to feel him lose control and savage her like she knew he desired.

Her eyesight shimmered as the images bombarded her. The colors of the room grew dim. *What the hell?* She glanced at his face to wake him, to find out what was happening, and saw that he was no longer asleep. His arm was above his head, resting on the pillow. His mouth was curved into a pleased smile. His glowing eyes stared back at her.

"You're beginning to change."

She pushed up onto one arm. "Change?" *Changing into what, a wolf?*

"That's exactly what I mean."

"Excuse me?" *How does he know what's going through my head?*

He ran a comforting hand down her arm, shoulder to wrist, and then back up again. The heat of his palm seeped into her bones. She exhaled on a sigh of contentment at the contact.

"Now that you have the wolf's soul melding with your own, I can hear you. Your thoughts."

That had her sitting up straight. His hand dropped and she missed it immediately, but she didn't reach to touch him. She didn't like the idea he could hear her thoughts. Not when she was still figuring things out with him. "I don't want you to read my thoughts."

Gideon chuckled and pulled her down next to him. He wrapped his arms around her and kissed her on the nose. "It's kind of my thing. Once you have a better handle on your wolf, you'll be able to keep most of your thoughts to yourself. Only when you want me to know will I."

She mulled over what he said. It made sense, she guessed. That still didn't make it any better. "What if I think something I'm not ready to let you know?"

"We'll deal with it, pixie, when the time comes." He kissed her softly before nuzzling her neck. His hot, wet tongue lapped at his mark. "Now, how about we get back to your exploring? I vote for lift."

She gasped and smacked him lightly on the chest. "You were listening."

"You weren't making it a secret. I'm more than happy to let you play. Lift the sheet and you'll see how much."

"You're like a horny sixteen-year-old."

"Yeah, but you like it."

She did, but he didn't need to know that. Ryder pushed against his shoulder, and she knew he let her roll him onto his back. She tossed to sheet back, exposing his naked body to her gaze.

Hot damn. She licked her lips, not knowing where to start. There were too many choices. His cock was filling right before her eyes. That happy trail of hair leading down from his belly button. His nipples hidden amongst the hair on his pecs.

Gideon chuckled and tucked his hands behind his head in an open invitation.

Crawling over him, she straddled his thighs. Her hands hovered over his chest. The slight tremble not

95

making her happy.

"Put them on me, Ryder. Touch me wherever you want."

Their gazes caught, his glowing brightly, full of banked heat. Her vision dulled, and she knew hers looked the same. Leaning forward, she placed her hands next to his head and kissed him. A soul-searing, earth-shattering kiss that left her breathless. Tongues tangled, dipped and dueled. He tasted like a warm summer night and crisp clean air. He tasted like...*hers*.

Blazing a path from his lips, she worked her way down his neck, hesitating on whether or not to go for the sweet spot. An itchy feeling formed beneath her skin. In her mind, a dark brown wolf paced back and forth. The image shocked her, stopping her exploration.

Gideon's hand cupped her cheek, forcing her to look up at him. "It's okay, Ryder. She's there with you. In your mind. Beneath your skin. But she isn't ready to mark yet. Like you, she needs to get to know me — my wolf — us."

She nodded and placed a kiss in the middle of his chest. Sifting her fingers through his chest hair, she found his nipples. Swirling her fingertips in smaller and smaller circles, the tips puckered. She pinched them at the same time and he groaned.

Against her belly, she felt his erection pulse, pushing up against the soft skin. Sliding down, she kissed and nipped him until she came face-to-face with his cock. His big, beautiful, hard cock that slick pre-cum dripped from. Sticking out her tongue, she lapped at the head, humming with satisfaction at the musky taste. Gideon jolted beneath her, bucking her up.

"Damn, pixie," he said.

"Need a warning next time?" She giggled, looking up the expanse of his body into his face. Teeth gritted, eyes narrowed, lust poured off him, swirling around her. It was intoxicating and powerful. He was putty in her hands.

Not bothering to wait for a reply, she licked the crown again before engulfing his shaft, sucking lightly. She kept her eyes focused on his face, soaking in his reaction. His eyes rolled and he hissed. His fingers curled into the sheets.

She smiled the best she could with a mouthful of cock. Working her way down, she licked and sucked. Over and over she fucked him with her mouth. Her intention was a little foreplay before climbing on top to ride. His hips came off the bed, thrusting into her mouth. He tried to dominate her from below. It was time to take back control. Hollowing out her cheeks, she came off him with a loud pop.

His eyes popped open, filled with question. She smirked and intentionally kept her mind blank. Crawling up his body, she put one hand by his head and used the other to grab his dick. She hovered over him for a second before dropping down, inch by agonizing inch. Her pussy clung to the thick erection tunneling in. Muscles contracted, tensing and relaxing.

"Oh shit, that feels good." This time her eyes rolled to the back of her head as she slid down. She rose slowly and dropped down again. Gideon's hands were on her waist, his big palms sliding onto her buttocks. His fingertips dug in as he grabbed on, helping her lift and fall. The slow leisurely pace picked up and soon he was fucking her from beneath, taking the control back. His hips snapped up, drilling into her. It was sensational, overwhelming, and oh so very right.

Finding her clit she pressed and rubbed. Tingles started in her feet, traveled up her legs, and she knew she was about to come. Leaning forward, Gideon tipped his head to the side, baring his throat to her. Her gums tingled with an edge of pain. Sliding her tongue over them, she found sharp, pointed fangs.

On instinct, as her orgasm hit, she sank her teeth into Gideon.

"Fuck yeah," he cried out, cupping the back of her head, keeping her pressed to his shoulder. He rolled them until she was on her back. It didn't matter that he'd taken over. His blood flowed into her mouth like melted dark chocolate. Decadent, rich, and smooth, she swallowed it down until he pulled away from her. "That's enough," he grunted, and she realized he'd stopped moving.

Gazing up at him, she saw something in his eyes. An emotion she didn't think he knew he was showing, and one she couldn't quite define. "Gideon?" she questioned, unsure of what was happening.

He opened his mouth, then closed it. The look on his face cleared. Dropping his forehead onto hers, he crooned softly. "Its okay, Ryder. It's all going to be fine."

"It will be if you start moving again." She wiggled her hips, making him grin. The strange mood lifted, and it seemed they both welcomed the change.

He pumped his hips, drawing out then ramming back in.

"Oh!" She squeaked in surprise.

"Like that?"

"Do it again," she demanded breathlessly.

He did, only this time grinding against her clit. A moan escaped her lips, and that was all it took for Gideon to start fucking her in earnest. He slammed his mouth down onto hers and within minutes, she was primed and ready to blow.

Gideon kissed over her jaw and down her neck. She turned her head, giving him her throat. He struck quickly, biting down on his mark, throwing her into orgasm. His name echoed off the walls. Four thrusts later he joined her, grinding out *mine* behind clenched teeth.

He collapsed on top of her, pressing all of that delicious weight on top of her. They wouldn't be able to stay like that long, but she'd soak it in while she could.

Too soon, he rolled slightly to the side, but didn't let her go. He pulled her into his body, blindly reached for the covers, and tossed them over their bodies. A soft kiss landed on the back of her head.

"I guess she was ready," he grumbled. "Back to sleep. You need rest."

She smiled into the pillow. "Yes, my Alpha," she said and yawned. She would happily stay in bed as long as he was with her.

CHAPTER THIRTEEN

March 21 – 9:30am

Gideon paced the living room floor, the soft carpet giving way beneath his booted feet. Fuck, he hated wearing shoes in the house. His wolf despised the footwear just as much. He knew it meant no impromptu shifting and running free. Something he enjoyed doing whenever possible. He doubted Ryder's parents would understand the need, so he opted for footwear.

Ryder was in the kitchen with his mother making the final preparations for breakfast. A feast that would feed at least fifty hungry people, more than enough for the eight, possibly ten people who would be in attendance. It was overkill, but Ryder's nervous energy needed harnessing.

It had spilled over onto his mother, and that was never a good thing. A nervous mother meant a hyper mother. While she meant well, his mom had a tendency to go bananas in the kitchen, which in this case wouldn't be a bad thing. There would be plenty of leftovers for the Pack later on.

After being told to steer clear of the main house,

Gideon knew there were some hurt feelings among the Pack. Food may not be the answer to that problem, but it sure as hell helped. Reactions to that bit of news ranged from disappointment to excitement. Many of them knew bringing in a human took longer than a shifter. Human families needed explanations and reassurances. Many of them made weekly trips to check on their newly turned family member. Some tried to whisk them away against their will, thinking distance would *cure* them.

Gideon stopped in his tracks, spinning until he had eyes on his mate. Would Ryder's parents try to take her away, keep her from him? She said she was the only daughter. Protected and loved by them all. If he had a daughter, he'd be pissed as hell if someone claimed to be her mate and wouldn't allow her to go home or visit. If he didn't have the balls to talk to Gideon face-to-face before sweeping his baby away, what kind of man was he?

Oh Shit! He would have a daughter — three of them. He may not have wanted a mate when they first met, but he'd be damned if he'd give her up now. He knew he had a life to come…with her. Laughter and love. Nights of passion that lead to lots of babies. What if she was already carrying his son? They hadn't used protection. It hadn't even crossed his mind. The wolf and the man demanded nothing stand between them. Ryder never mentioned it either.

Mine, his wolf roared, the human agreeing completely. Gideon's fangs dropped and a growl broke free of his chest. Ryder looked up from the cutting board, knife stilled mid-chop and smiled. A pretty blush stole across her cheeks the longer he stared. He knew his eyes glowed with possession, reminding her of their lovemaking. His mother asked her a question and she quickly looked away.

Gideon couldn't though. He had to keep her in his sight. Fear skated down his spine at the thought of losing her. At her leaving his home — no, their home. A large hand dropped onto his stiff shoulder, surprising him. "It'll be okay, Gideon. That woman isn't going anywhere."

Gideon peeled his eyes away from Ryder to look at his father. "How can you be so sure? What if her parents insist on it? What if they try to drag her away, and forbid her to be with me?"

An amused smile lit up his dad's face. "I get the feeling Ryder isn't the kind of girl to let her parents dictate what she does. She was on a solo trip in the Grand Canyon, for God's sake. If her parents had been in charge of her life, they never would have let her go."

"Why do you say that?"

"Because, if she were my daughter, I wouldn't let her go either."

Gideon's gaze drifted back to Ryder, a small smile tilting his lips. "Her dad tried to buy her out of it. Said he'd reimburse her the money she'd already put into the trip if she didn't go. She refused."

His dad chuckled. "She's strong-willed. You'll need that in a Luna."

Gideon snorted, some of his tension evaporating. "I'd call it stubborn."

"Whatever you want to call it, I don't think you need to worry. Besides, I have the feeling that girl is seconds away from falling in love with you, just like you're falling in love with her. They won't be able to tear you two apart."

Gideon's head snapped back in shock. "Excuse me? I am *not* in love with her," he hissed out. He looked to see if Ryder heard what he said. Thankfully, she hadn't. Her head was tipped back and she was laughing. Joy and happiness radiated from her. The slender column of her throat made his gums tingle with the need to mark her again. The bite he'd put there earlier peeked out of her shirt, letting everyone know the claim he had on her.

His dad eased his bulky frame onto the arm of the couch, crossing his arms across his chest. "I said *falling* in love."

It didn't matter *what* his father said. Falling in love meant *being* in love. He couldn't—it was too soon. He'd just gotten out of a relationship. He wasn't ready, was he? Didn't he need time to get over—shit? He couldn't even remember his ex-girlfriend's name. He waited for the panic to well in his chest, for his breath to clog his lungs. It didn't happen though. "We just met," he said lamely.

His father rolled his eyes, but didn't say a word.

Gideon's brother didn't have a problem voicing his opinion. Forrest, who'd been asleep on the couch, rolled to his feet, stretched his arms and yawned. "That's dumb. It shouldn't matter how long you've known her. Your mate is your mate. Everyone knows you should fall in love with your mate. It's a given. She's the other half of you and your wolf. She completes a part of you that's been missing. I'm going to guess it's your sense of humor. That's been missing for years." Forrest scuttled away, laughing before Gideon could grab him. He dashed into the kitchen, disrupting Ryder and their mom.

Ryder looked at him, her smile instantly dropping. Whatever she saw in his face had her coming to him. Her tiny arms looped around his waist, and she squeezed him tight. Getting up on her tiptoes, she kissed him before stepping away.

"What was that for?" He asked, grabbing her hand so she couldn't get too far. The need to touch her was strong.

She shrugged, her attention riveted on something outside the big bay window. "It felt like you needed it."

Gideon stilled, his heart stopping in his chest. She could feel him? He went to ask what she meant when she let out an excited shriek.

"There's Dad's truck, and it looks like my brother Cameron is following him. Oh my god, I think they *all* came."

Gideon's entire family crowded around the front window, watching a big black truck and a silver SUV pull

103

up in the circle drive. Ryder's hand tightened around his, and he felt her anxiety ratchet up a notch. Pulling her close, he wrapped his arms around her. She melted into him, her shoulders relaxing immediately. "It'll be okay," he said, infusing as much confidence into the words as he could. She needed him even if she didn't say it.

*****

Ryder tried her damndest not to fidget as she waited for her family to mount the massive stairs that led to the front doors. Gideon stood behind her, stroking her arms, his solid presence keeping her calm. "What the hell is taking them so long? It isn't like they have to hike five miles to get from the drive to the front door," she huffed out impatiently.

"Do you want to open the door and wait for them?" he said softly, his voice caressing her ears. A shiver raced down her spine, and the ever-present arousal she experienced around him snaked through her blood. It was like that any time she was near him, and growing stronger by the minute. It had to be the markings. He'd bitten her four times and, according to him, there was one more to go. The final bite, which would bind them together forever.

She didn't know what had bothered him earlier, but she knew something was wrong. She was done second-guessing the urge to soothe and comfort him. They both felt better when they touched. A slight brush of a hand. Thighs pressed together while eating. It didn't matter how as long as it happened. She loved it. Loved the feelings that wrapped around her and made her feel whole. Like at that very moment. "No. I don't want them to think I need rescuing if I fling myself at them."

He chuckled, the vibrations reverberating through her chest. "And why would you fling yourself at them?"

She tipped her head back to capture his attention. "You need to understand. This is the *longest* I've been away from them. Four days. That's nothing in the grand scheme of things. And even though I don't live at home and haven't for five years, I still saw them every day at work, or when I popped over to the house. Now, I'm about to tell them I'm not coming home—ever. I'm not coming back to work. And I'm moving in with a man I met three days ago." She paused as something rather important dawned on her. "You do want me to move in, right?"

"Yes, my Luna. I need you here with me."

A grin split her face. "Good, because it was going to happen regardless."

A worried expression crossed his face. "When did you get the impression I was keeping you captive? You can visit your family whenever you want."

"I like being held captive by you," she said, wiggling her hips.

Gideon spun her before dropping a quick kiss on her lips. "Oh pixie, the things we can do," he whispered, lust threading through his deep voice.

She chuckled. "I'm sure, Alpha." Running her hands up his chest and around to his nape, she threaded her fingers together and tugged him down. Catching his bottom lip between her teeth, she nipped him and let go.

The doorbell rang, stopping them from an all out make-out session. It was a good thing Gideon's parents couldn't see them either. Not that they seemed to care. The overly affectionate wolves were constantly touching each other.

Spinning out of his arms, Ryder threw the door open. "Daddy," she squealed and launched herself at him.

"Hey there, girly." Kissing her on the cheek, he set her down.

Ryder turned to her mom, enveloping her in a hug. "Hey, Mom." She felt Gideon behind her, silently watching them all. Stepping away from her mom, she backed up and ushered them in. Cameron, Nathan, and Jonathan followed their parents inside, not one of them saying a word.

Closing the front door, she grabbed Gideon's hand. "Come into the living room and I'll introduce everyone."

When they entered the living room, Gideon's family was standing, welcoming smiles on their faces. Stephan had his arm around Julie. Forrest stood to the side.

Her family stopped and Gideon and Ryder ended up in the middle. She looked between the two families and giggled. It was like an old western showdown, both families waiting to see what the other would do.

Gideon slid his hand down her back and looked down at her, eyebrow raised in question. She didn't know why he was letting her run the show. He was the damn Alpha. Just because it was her family didn't mean he couldn't take the lead. "All right then. Sparks clan, this is Deckard clan. The handsome man next to me is Gideon. We met a couple days ago…"

"A couple days ago?" her father interrupted. "Weren't you on a hiking trip a couple days ago, young lady?" His eyes narrowed in that fatherly you-better-tell-me-the-truth way.

Ryder's mom put a hand on her father's arm, a soft smile tilting her lips. "Drake, let your daughter finish the introductions."

"You're in so much trouble, brat," Jonathan sing-songed softly.

Gideon stiffened next to her, and turned an angry glare on Jon. Jon stepped back slightly, bumping into Nate, who shook his head and rolled his eyes.

Ryder snorted. "Whatever, jerk," she replied cheekily to her youngest brother.

Forrest laughed and covered it up with a cough, earning him a disapproving frown from his father. Ryder had a feeling Forrest and Jon would get along well.

"Go ahead, Ryder," her mom said with an encouraging smile.

"This is Gideon's family: his dad Stephan, mom Florence, and younger brother Forrest. Deckards, this is my family. My dad Drake, mom Julie, my two older brothers Cam and Nate, and the baby, Jon."

Everyone stood around in awkward silence until Ryder's mom broke it. She stepped toward Florence and folded her into a hug. "It is so nice to meet you." Florence smiled and returned the hug. After that, everyone moved in and shook hands.

Gideon wrapped his arms around her from behind and squeezed. "See, I told you it would be okay," he whispered next to her ear. Louder he said, "Let's head into the dining room. Ryder and Mom have been busy all morning getting a breakfast feast ready. I'm sure you all must be starving. We can sit and talk once we've had our fill."

CHAPTER FOURTEEN

March 21 – 11:00am

Gideon rested his hand on top of Ryder's, hoping to calm her down. Her leg bounced beneath the table, and she'd barely taken a bite of food. It had been an hour since they all sat down. Bits of small talk went on between the families as they ate.

Forrest and Jon sat across from each other arguing over the best tactics to use on some level of a first-person shooter video game they both played. Ryder's older brothers, Cam and Nate, occasionally butted in with advice, but it was clear the younger men deemed it unworthy of consideration.

The moms talked recipes for big families, and the dads more or less surveyed what was happening, adding their two cents here and there. Gideon knew they would have to talk about what was going on soon.

He got the impression Ryder's mom knew more about the situation than she was letting on. She smiled softly at her daughter and him, then would sigh happily.

Ryder turned her hand over and threaded their fingers together. She sighed, but her leg bounced even more. Pushing his chair back some, he tugged on her hand, pulling her from her chair. He hauled her onto his lap, and only then did she begin to relax.

Drake cleared his throat and looked pointedly at them. Ryder blushed and tried to move. Gideon wasn't having it. She was uptight and nervous. He knew his touch would be a balm to her. She needed him and he needed her. Her father would have to get over it.

"Hey, brat, want to tell us what's going on?" Jon had leaned forward to look their way. His brows were furrowed slightly in concern.

"Jonathan Graham, you stop calling your sister brat right this second," Julie scolded.

Gideon couldn't hide his grin when Ryder stuck her tongue out at her brother, and quickly pulled it back into her mouth when her mom looked their way. The picture of innocence…his mate.

"What is going on, Ryder?" her father asked, sitting back in his chair, arms crossed over his big chest.

"I can answer that, dear. Ryder has found the *One,* and if I'm not mistaken, he's a shifter."

Drake's head whipped in his wife's direction, then back at them. "What?" he bellowed. "She's only been gone four days. How can she have…wait…what?"

Gideon's dad and mom stiffened in their seats, preparing to jump up to protect them. Gideon didn't think that would be necessary. Ryder's mom was too blasé about it all.

"Oh, do calm down, Drake. It was bound to happen to someone in my family," Julie grinned and patted her husband on the arm. "I told you that when we first started dating. It isn't my fault you forgot things in your old age."

That was when all hell broke loose. Julie was peppered with questions from everyone. Her husband and boys. Gideon's mom and dad. Ryder sat on Gideon's lap as still as a statue. Her breathing turned shallow, pulse picked up. Confusion and excitement rolled off her.

He tuned in to her in his mind, hoping to capture the thoughts running through her head. He knew he wouldn't be able to talk to her through the connection, however. Not until her first shift and their wolves met in person. When he didn't hear anything, he turned her head with a finger on the chin.

"You okay, pixie?"

"She knew," she said, clearly surprised.

"Seems that way. I take it she never said anything to you kids."

"Nope. But you know, she didn't freak out when I told her my roommate was a fox-shifter. She was actually pleased about it."

"Interesting. Mind if I try a little experiment?"

Ryder shrugged. "Go ahead. Wait. What are you going to do? Will it hurt them?"

Gideon grinned and kissed her on the lips, because he could and she was too enticing. "Just going to let a little power out. See if it affects any of them."

"Will I feel it?"

"You should, but not in a painful way like what happens to my brother. From what I've been told, it might turn you on," his voice deepened with arousal. The Alpha power would be like a warm caress from him over her entire body, like he was touching every inch of her soft, smooth skin all at the same time. A total and complete assault on her body. He would feel her reaction and smell her blossoming arousal. Holy fuck, it made his palms itch to do just that, and his dick was hard as hell.

She apparently noticed his rising dilemma. Her eyes opened wide as she wiggled on his lap. "Oh my," she giggled quietly. "Do it."

Gideon called to the power within, unleashing it on the unsuspecting guests. A soft, almost transparent mist formed around him. Pushing it outward with his mind, it rolled over everyone like a heated wave.

"Damn it, Gideon," Forrest whined, dipping his head low.

His mother and father, bowed slightly, not nearly as affected by it because he was their offspring. Giving birth to an Alpha had to have some perks.

Nate cringed and Jon let out a low groan. Drake, Julie, and Cam glanced around the table, confusion clearly written on their faces.

It took every ounce of willpower Gideon had in him to focus on what happened to the rest of the people in the room. Having his mate feel the Alpha power was as intoxicating as he'd been told. Ryder's body was a flame of pure need. He felt her craving to have his hands and lips on her. The need to have her womanly channel filled with his cock. Her natural floral scent mixed with that of her sweet arousal. It wafted up into his nostrils, filling his chest. She moaned in his ear, running a hand over his chest, and cupped his face. She nipped his earlobe and licked around the outer shell. "Need you," she whispered hungrily.

Gideon gritted his teeth to keep from turning his head and marking her in front of her family. She was on the edge of an orgasm. His bite would push her over and have her crying out his name. He didn't think that would go over very well right at the moment. Tightening his hold on her, he kissed her swiftly. "Soon, pixie. We have your family here right now."

Leaning away from him, she blinked rapidly. "Oh!"

He extinguished the power flowing from him, and it

111

promptly released those captured in the thrall.

"What the fuck just happened?" Nate groused, shaking his head.

Jon scrubbed his hands over his face. "Hell if I know, but Cam didn't seem bothered."

"I don't have a clue what you're whining about," Cam grunted and looked at his parents. "You guys seem fine."

Gideon took a deep breath. "Mrs. Sparks is correct. We're shifters, wolves."

"You can call me Julie."

Gideon nodded and smiled at her, relaxing slightly. If she were in their corner, it would go over a hell of a lot easier. "I let my Alpha power out. I was curious to see if any of you would react. Ryder did because she's my mate. Nate and Jon did as well. It would seem they have the shifter gene in them. Cam doesn't and neither do you Mr. and Mrs. Sparks."

"Holy shit," Jon exclaimed. "That's fucking cool." Cam popped him on the back of the head, making him grunt.

"Jonathan," Drake warned.

"Sorry, Dad."

"Julie, do you mind clueing us all in?" Gideon's mom asked.

Julie Sparks pushed her plate away and picked up her coffee cup. She settled back in her chair and by the time she was ready to start talking, everyone was focused on her. It would be easier that way. She was excited and scared to hear what her husband and children had to say. She and Drake had never talked about it after that first time. In the first blush of their romance, they pushed it to the back of their minds. It never dawned on her to have the kids tested. She just assumed it would all work out in

112

the wash. It had been a while since someone in her family changed over.

She turned to her husband first. Gathering up his hand she said, "You completely forgot when I told you there was a shifter in my ancestors, didn't you?"

Drake looked at her, his brows furrowed in thought. He was still the handsomest man she'd ever met. His blond hair was now a light brown and sprinkled with grey. She waited as he thought back, could see him processing her words, and was pleased when a slow grin curled up the corner of his mouth. "I remember, Love bug. Quite a few generations back one of your grandparents was a shifter."

"Right and he had a child with a non-shifter. That child, a female, inherited the shifter gene. Mitochondrial Inheritance. After that, the women of the family all become carriers and passed the gene down generation after generation. It didn't mean someone would be a shifter, but there was a possibility they could be mated to one. It seems that three of our children have inherited the shifter gene."

"Huh, I feel oddly left out," murmured Cameron.

"Dude, you wouldn't have wanted to feel him flexing his muscle on you, trust me," Nate reassured his brother. "It's weird."

Cameron smirked and Julie knew it would be okay. "I never did like to bow down to anyone else."

"I'm sorry I never talked to you kids about it. I just—it didn't cross my mind. I would have talked to you about it, Ryder once you got serious with a boy, but you never did."

"Until now," Ryder quipped.

"Yes, a little late to have that talk now." Julie said ruefully. "I see his mark, sweetheart. You've already let him claim you."

Two things happened then that Julie didn't think through.

Drake squeezed her hand tightly, only letting up when she yelped.

Ryder blushed a crimson red. All eyes turned in her direction, and Julie could have kicked herself for bringing that up.

Her daughter, never one to cower, straightened her shoulders, and her head tilted up a notch. "Yes, I have. I belong with Gideon, and I didn't see a reason not to let him claim me."

Julie saw Gideon tighten his hold on Ryder. She leaned into him and sighed softly. They were meant for each other.

"I'm glad. All I want is for you to be happy."

"Thanks, mom." Ryder scrambled from Gideon's lap and made a beeline for her. Julie jumped up from her chair and hugged her. A tear slipped free as the knowledge that her baby was moving on filtered into her brain.

Ryder stepped back and turned to her father. Drake stood and engulfed his daughter in a hug.

Julie was surprised when Gideon gathered her into his arms and squeezed her tight.

"I'll take good care of her," he promised, and she knew he would. Fate wouldn't have it any other way.

CHAPTER FIFTEEN

March 21 – Noon

Gideon closed the refrigerator and looked around the kitchen. The last of the food had been wrapped, and the dishes were in the dishwasher. His mother was brewing a pot of coffee in the industrial machine they broke out for gatherings. Julie was stacking scones on a plate. Now that everything was out in the open, the women acted as if they'd known each other forever and not a mere couple of hours.

"We're going to join Drake and your father in the library. It'll be quiet in there and we won't be interrupted while we're talking," his mother said, knowing he would question what their plan was. Filling a large carafe with coffee and placing it next to the cups on a serving tray, she brushed a kiss across his cheek. "You kids stay out of trouble," she called out as she left, Ryder's mom following on her heels.

"Jon and I are going to fire up the video console. I'll finally have someone that knows what the hell he's doing with a controller."

"I told you I sucked when you bought that game. I'm sure one of the pups around here would have played those missions with you." Gideon didn't know why his brother demanded he help him out. All Gideon had done was get Forrest killed over and over again.

"The pups aren't allowed in my game room and you know it. The one time I let them in, a controller ended up embedded in the wall and someone chewed on the couch. Seriously, who does shit like that?"

"I remember," he replied. They'd had to re-cover the couch just so he didn't have to listen to his brother bitch about it.

"I like to play," Ryder piped up, and he almost groaned out loud. The last thing he wanted was to spend the afternoon with their brothers. His plans involved getting her naked and marking her again.

"Hell no, brat," Jon retorted. "You're horrible." Jon looked at Forrest. "All she does is make her character stand around and talk about the scenery. She likes to stop and try to read the signs and posters."

Forrest laughed and Ryder stuck her tongue out at them.

"We need to get going, Ryder." Cam said, coming up to hug her. "I don't know what to think about all of this, but if you're happy…it's okay with me." He shrugged and passed her off to her other brother, Nate.

"I think it explains a lot about me," Nate said. "But he better treat you right." Nate gave him the stink eye, and Gideon had to keep from rolling his eyes at him. That boy wouldn't be able to take Gideon on his best day. Gideon was older, stronger, and wiser.

"You work with a woman named Donna, right?" Gideon asked, in order to change the topic.

Nate grinned. "Yeah. She one of yours?"

Gideon's brow dropped into a frown. The way he said *yours* could be taken too many ways. He wouldn't stand for anyone insulting a Pack member.

"A wolf," Nate clarified.

"Yeah. She's a pure bred shifter. Her family has been with the Pack for generations."

"She's hot," Nate remarked. "*Really* hot." His mouth curved into a knowing smile. Gideon shook his head. He didn't think Nate would know what to do with Donna even if given the chance.

"I'm so totally telling her," Ryder snickered behind him. "She thinks you're a butt."

Nate's eyes bugged out and he turned, trying to grab her. "Come here, brat."

Ryder spun away and laughed. Nate took chase, but didn't have a chance in hell of catching her. The triggered shifter genes increased her speed, agility, and strength. She ducked around Cam in a blur, and rounded the corner of the big island in the kitchen. Nate stopped in his tracks and tried to reverse direction. The second he got close, only because she let him, she jumped on top of the counter and vaulted over, dashing into the living room. Her peel of laughter filled the space as she made her way through the house. Nate stood stupefied at what had happened. Ryder came back into the kitchen from a different direction, jumping into Gideon's arms. She wrapped her limbs around him, giggling with utter joy.

Cam laughed and a defeated Nate shook his head. "Don't say a word, brat. See ya' later." Cam ushered his brother out and they left.

"What now, pixie?" He rumbled out. He felt her blood coursing through her veins, and his wolf pushing at him to taste her again. Gideon didn't have a problem with that. He craved her taste on his lips.

"We're all alone," she said, licking her lips. Lust flared

in the depths of her eyes, turning them gold. He knew her wolf was pressing to the front.

"Not quite, but it can be arranged. Think you can keep your voice down?"

"Let's find out," she leaned forward and showered kisses all over his face.

Gideon groaned when her plump little lips captured his earlobe. "Hold that thought," he said.

He put out a mental call to his Beta. It didn't take long for his friend to show up. He walked into the kitchen cautiously. His head rearing back when he saw them tangled up.

"Alpha." Diego dipped his head in respect.

"Hey, Diego," Ryder said, not the least bit surprised by his presence or embarrassed by the situation.

"Uh, Luna," he replied. "I can call you that now, can't I?"

"I guess." She leaned back slightly and stared Gideon in the face. "Or is there some ceremony I need to go through first?"

Gideon smiled at his mate. Her instincts about being a wolf were on point. "There will be an official naming after the last marking, but you *are* my Luna."

He could tell she was thinking that bit of information over. There was so much she needed to learn. So much she needed to know. "Okay." She looked over her shoulder at Diego. "We'll go with Luna or Ryder. Whatever is appropriate at the time."

A sense of satisfaction filled him hearing her gift his best friend with that privilege. She could demand he call her Luna and only Luna. His ex-girlfriend had tried that and failed. The ease with which Ryder operated within the Pack the last couple of days proved she was a natural in her position.

Diego nodded adoringly at her. "Thank you, Luna." He turned his attention to Gideon. He schooled his features, the mask of being his second falling into place. "What is it you needed, Alpha?"

"Our parents are in the library. Forrest and Ryder's brother Jon are gaming. I'm taking my mate upstairs. I need you to watch over everything while we're," he cleared his throat, "otherwise occupied. There's food for the Pack in the fridge."

"Of course, Alpha."

"Later Diego," Ryder called out as Gideon strode from the kitchen, his mate wrapped lovingly around his body.

He took the steps two at a time. Slamming the door shut behind him, he strode straight to the bed, spun and fell back with Ryder still glued to his front.

"In a bit of a hurry?" She queried, dropping kisses all over his face.

"And you aren't?" He pushed her shirt up her torso; flinging it over the side of the bed once it cleared her head. Her satin-covered breasts pressed into his chest as she attacked him with renewed gusto.

"I can't get enough of you," she puffed out breathlessly, scooting down his body. Lips and fingers blazed a trail over his skin. She fingered the flat disks on his chest, plucking and pulling until his nipples stood up. Flicking a nail across each one, he jolted, bucking his hips up. The electric shock he'd felt racing to his groin. "You like that," she crowed and did it again.

Gideon's answer was to grunt. His hands itched to feel her skin beneath his palms. To massage and grope each and every inch of her. He unhooked her bra, sliding the straps over her smooth shoulders. She sat up; let it drop, then sent it sailing in the same direction as her shirt. He knew his mouth was hanging open at the sight. His hands were on her pert breasts before the bra even cleared the bed.

119

He pulled her down, taking turns sucking her nipples into his mouth. Ryder grunted and groaned as he wrapped his tongue around the turgid peaks. She ground against his throbbing erection, riding him hard. The seam of her borrowed jeans gliding over the head of his denim-clad dick, seemingly rubbing her in just the right spot. Her breath hitched slightly before she mewled. Her orgasm tightening her body like the string on a bow. Her back arched, head thrown back. His name a breathy prayer.

"You're fucking gorgeous when you come." Gideon rolled her over, stripped them both of their clothes and was back on top of her in a matter of seconds. He'd wanted to take his time with her. *Planned* on taking his time, but that shit wasn't going to happen. When he'd pulled down her jeans and skimpy panties, her arousal wafted up, flooding his senses and overpowering all of his good intentions.

Without finesse he thrust into her, pulling groans from each of them. She was wet and tight. Her pussy contracted around his cock. Sucking it in further. Daring him to try and pull out. He needed this connection with every fiber of his being. There had been a time when he'd turned his nose down at this elemental thing he felt for her. Now — he needed it like he needed his next breath. He needed her.

He ghosted his lips over her collarbone, waiting for her to tilt her head. She didn't take long either. He licked his mark. The one he placed on her delicate skin where neck and shoulder met. Her breath hitched and he rocked his hips slightly. Thrusting just enough to make her gasp his name. He was testing her, teasing her to see her reaction. She submitted without thought. A swell of emotion rose in his chest. One he didn't want to look at too closely. It couldn't be anything more than possession. She was his mate, and she didn't fight him on it.

She rolled her hips, matching his thrusts as he sped up. Pulling out until the cockhead barely breached her hot opening before sliding home. They kept the rhythm easy but intense; it didn't take long before he needed more.

Gideon pulled out and away. Grabbing her by the waist and flipping her over. "Get on all fours," he growled, the wolf pushing to the surface.

Ryder scrambled into position, tossing a look of excited lust over her shoulder. Her eyes glowed brighter than before and, with their gazes locked, he slammed into her. His wolf demanded blood. Demanded a melding of spirits on the ether one more time. Hands tightly gripping her hips, his claws extended, digging in marginally. Instead of a cry of pain, Ryder moaned, her eyes fluttering shut.

He took her hard, rocking in and out of her tight sheath. The smack of skin on skin echoed in the room. Musk filled the air around them. Her inner muscles quivering, her breath quickened. She chanted his name over and over.

It was time.

Gideon released his Alpha power, calling to his Luna. Mist swirled around them as heat ebbed and flowed. She gasped and he felt the power caress her body like a physical touch. Her pussy creamed, becoming slicker than before. It eased his relentless tunneling into her receptive body.

Leaning over her back, she tilted her head to the side, giving him access to his mark. This would be the marking that bonded them for life. The fifth and final mark linking them for all eternity. On a roar, he sank his teeth in triggering her orgasm. She screamed his name, thrusting back into him, the spasms of her pussy pulling him into oblivion with her.

Gideon collapsed on top of Ryder, sprawling them both out. He rolled and pulled her with him. Tucking her close to his overheated body. Wolf and man needed her like never before. "Goddamn," he murmured into her hair.

"I'll say," she laughed lightly. "Couldn't stay quiet. I hope your room is soundproof."

"It's not." And damn if that didn't make him happy. He wanted everyone to know she belonged to him. That she cried *his* name out in satisfaction.

"Damn, my parents are gonna freak. I won't be able to look at them without blushing."

Gideon stroked a hand down her arm. "It'll be fine, Luna. You're mom seems to know a bit more about shifter culture than she let on. I don't doubt she'll calm your dad down."

Ryder rolled over to face him, stroking a finger down his face. "That'll be awkward," she said in a hushed tone before kissing him.

Gideon hummed in reply, too busy enjoying her lips against his to verbally agree. An electric snap in his head caught his attention. He focused on it, and heard Ryder in his head. *Love you, Gideon.*

He held his breath, waiting for fear and panic to flood him. It was the second time that it didn't. Instead, joy filled his heart and his wolf sang. He placed a bruising kiss on her lips, pouring everything he felt into it. Pulling away only when his lungs burned, deprived of much needed oxygen. "I love you too, Ryder."

A soft smile lifted her kiss-swollen lips. "I know."

EPILOGUE

March 31st

Ryder flew down the stairs and rushed to the front door. Whoever was out there was smashing on the button like they'd never touched one before. The echo of the chimes going off had the younger wolves, which were hanging out with Forrest, howling in the lower level game room. The guy was going to have a cow if one of them ripped into the couch again. It had taken her all of thirty minutes to get Forrest to allow the younger generation of the Pack back into his sanctuary.

Flinging the door open, she was shocked to her toes to see the two Rangers from the Backcountry Information Center who'd given her the permit almost two weeks ago. The tall blond man stood behind the leggy brunette woman. Hands stuffed into the pocket of his cargo pants, his eyes were glued to the woman's ass. She snorted and drew the man's attention. One side of his mouth cocked up and mischief glittered in his gaze.

There was definitely something going on between those two. But what the hell were they doing at Gideon's place? "Hi," she said. "Is there something I can help you with?" Ryder looked between the Rangers. The woman looked back at the man, who shrugged.

"I'm only here because she's here," he said.

"Well darlin', I just wanted to check on ya'. The shuttle driver told us you never did show up for your ride, so I was concerned," the brunette beamed a dazzling smile at Ryder.

"Okay, but how did you know I was *here*? I don't live here." Ryder tightened her grip on the doorknob, ready to slam the door in their faces.

"Yes, you do," Gideon boomed behind her. His voice flowed out strong and demanding, rippling over her senses. In four days time, on April 4th, she would experience her first shift. The closer it got to the date, the more aware of her senses she became. She could feel Gideon's wolf within him attempting to lure her wolf out. It made for some fantastic foreplay. The poor man (not really, what guy thought it was horrible to have a woman throwing herself at him) had to have his Beta Diego take over the duties of running the Pack during this week before her shift.

Every chance she got; she was rubbing herself against her mate, horny as hell and in a near constant state of readiness. The straw that broke Gideon's control was when she climbed into his lap during a Pack meeting and damn near let everyone have a free show. He had no intention of letting anyone see her in the throes of passion. As far as he was concerned, that was for his eyes only.

Gideon walked up behind her and wrapped an arm across her chest. He tugged her back until she leaned into him. "Can I help you?" Gideon asked, a layer of steel vibrating in his voice.

The blond guy — *damn, what was his name again* — stepped up next to the woman. "Chloe wanted to make sure your mate was fine after missing her scheduled shuttle pick-up. One of your Pack, Donna I believe, told us she was here. Chloe wanted to see for herself."

Ryder relaxed and let go of the door. "Thank you," she said, smiling at the woman. "I had a little accident and Gideon rescued me."

Chloe's eyebrow went up and she smirked. She looked at her co-worker, then back at them. "So, ya'll found a love match in the canyon. That is so sweet," she drawled.

Ryder couldn't help the grin on her face from widening. "I guess we did. It must have been fate. Would you like to come in?"

"Thank you, but no." The blond, Cupert (ah ha!), draped his arm across Chloe's shoulders. The beautiful brunette blushed a deep red. "We need to get back to work. Got a big day tomorrow." He winked and turned, taking Chloe with him. They strode away, walking down the long drive.

"I wonder where they parked?"

"No idea and I don't care." Gideon spun her. Picked her up. Then tossed her over his shoulder. It seemed she wasn't the only one with a constant craving for her mate.

Chloe and Eros waited until they were out of view before disappearing. They reappeared right outside of Chloe's home, their human realm clothing gone and in its place the garments of their world. Damn, Eros would miss seeing Chloe in those tight cargo pants. They molded to her ass perfectly, accentuating her firm, heart-shaped rear. He'd had more than one elicit dream featuring that luscious body part.

"I told you they were in love," Chloe gloated. She crossed her arms under her breasts, plumping them up. It was a hell of a view.

"Neither of them actually said so," Eros countered. He had to keep this about the couple and not about how much he wanted to toss her over *his* shoulder and find a luxuriously padded place to have his wicked way with her.

Chloe rolled her eyes. "Anyone could see just by looking at them that they are. You mean to tell me that you, the ultimate authority on love, desire, and romance, couldn't see it?"

Eros inched closer, brushing his bare chest against hers. Damn, even that slight contact was excruciatingly delightful. His cock filled behind the wisp of fabric now hanging on his waist. He may need to find a way to bring those damn cargo pants back to his realm. They, at least, hid his condition from prying eyes more than the wrap did. "I'm only stating a fact. Neither said to *us*...they were in love."

"But you aren't denying that they are?"

Eros pressed a little closer. Their lips a fraction apart from one another. Chloe's tongue drifted over her lower lip, brushing against his. He caught the shiver that skated over her body even as he repressed his own. "I'm not," he said. "I'm willing to give you a reward too. You've matched three couples. Three more than I thought you'd be able to manage," he smirked.

This close he got a firsthand look at the fire sparking in her eyes. The deep brown hue turned to liquid gold. Her lips pursed, inadvertently, he assumed, pressing against his in the barest of contact. It was enough to pull a gasp from her.

There was no way Eros could hold back any longer. His hands came up. One cupping the back of her head. The other wrapping around her waist, pulling her flush to his overheated body. He drove his tongue into her mouth, tasting every inch. She moaned and her hands came up, nails digging into his pectoral muscles. The kiss went on and on, until he had no choice but to let go or pass the fuck out from lack of oxygen.

He released Chloe and stepped back. Pulling an

unaffected look on his face, he waited until the glazed look of lust faded from hers. "I'll see you tomorrow at the Parthenon. Same time as before." Spinning, he strode away, putting as much distance between them as quickly as possible without actually running.

Being around Chloe challenged every aspect of his control. Curbing his need for instant gratification was sweeter than the most decadent ambrosia he'd ever had.

Three months down, nine to go. For the love of Zeus, he hoped he could last that long before having her completely at his mercy.

THE END

Thank you for reading Gideon and I hope you enjoyed the story. Please consider leaving a review at your eStore of choice. Feedback is always much appreciated.

Lisa, Book 4, will be releasing April 3rd

Thane: January

Mystic Zodiac, Book 1

Fallen Angel Thane has been exiled to the realm of humans and Mystics for almost fifty years after what he considers a slight *misunderstanding*, too bad Zeus didn't agree. After the blush of exile wears off, Thane dedicates his new life to helping those in need, all in the hope of impressing the imposing God.

A visit from his Watcher with one more task sets Thane up to finally get what he's dreamed about for decades... his rightful place back on Olympus with his brothers. All he needs to do is keep one woman from "doing something stupid." He determined to ignore his body responding for the first time in almost fifty years in order to go home.

Amara Hope is desperate to bring her brother home, traveling into the heart of Viral City day after day putting her life at risk. As her last living relative, he's all she has left. When a hunky Good Samaritan grudgingly offers help, she's all too willing to accept. Once they get her brother home and begin spending more time together, the more Amara knows he's the one for her.

What the two don't know is that the Gods are playing games with their lives, and they're on a collision course with love.

Word Count: 32,299

Parvati: February

Mystic Zodiac, Book 2

Parvati Shiva, a true descendent of the Goddess of love and devotion, is fed up. She runs a successful dating site, connecting Mystics and humans all over the world with their one true love. The only she hasn't been able to find love for is…her.

When a hacker gets into her network and website, shutting down her site in the height of the busy season, she calls on her cousin Jag for help, who in turn reaches out to an old friend.

Colin Patterson, IT guru and confirmed bachelor, quickly agrees to help his friend's sister out with her computer problem, hoping it will be a long drawn out process. He's eager to escape his mother's matchmaking Valentine's Day party. She's invited all of the single women — and a few men — to jump-start his dating life, something he has no interest in at all.

One mistaken identity later, Colin ruins his chance with the beautiful Indian woman he's instantly attracted to. Will he be able to prove he isn't a boss bashing idiot, save Parvati's company, and win her affections before he doesn't have a reason to stick around?

Warning: This book contains a geeky hero who can't keep his mouth shut, a strong willed businesswoman dealing in love, and an attraction that neither can deny.

Please note: **This book has a hot M/M scene.**

Word Count: 26,817

Currently available in ebook only

Shifted Plans
Shifter U, Book 1

Decadent Publishing

Avery Hillman has one year of college left. Once it's over she has plans, BIG plans. A job managing her family's medical practice, an apartment of her own, and a new life where she's the one in charge. No hovering family, no annoying siblings, and no mate to have to divide her time to be with.

Declan Weller has one more class to finish. One more thing he can cross off his ten-year plan. Once that is done, he can transfer to the new job waiting for him and his new life. He isn't looking for his mate and as far as he's concerned, finding her can wait another two years.

The Fates have a plan of their own. One that includes throwing Avery and Declan in each other's path. It's high time those two found each other and learn the most important thing of all…sometimes plans need to shift.

~~~~~

Genre: Paranormal Romance, New Adult, Shifters
Featuring Lion Shifters

Available in ebook and print

Craving More
Tiger Nip, Book 1

TEZ Publishing

Corrine Hart is ready for few days off for rest and relaxation. At the top of her to-do list is spending as much time as possible in tiger form and doing her best to banish all thoughts of the mysterious Hunky Cupcake Guy who spent the last two weeks driving her libido insane.

Jett Montgomery-Murphy just wants to know if the tasty treats that keep showing up at work are the same ones his best friend used to get while they were in college. A trip out to Sweet Confections confirms what he thought and brings him in close contact with the one woman he's secretly lusted after for years, his best friend's sister Corrine.

A late night tryst leads to two tigers finding their mates and two humans unsure what to do next. Add in an overbearing brother, a best friend with her own drama, and a crazy ex-girlfriend that has a checkered past and you have a recipe for disaster.

Will Corrine and Jett be able to overcome the unexpected obstacles on their way to falling in love? Or will they throw in the towel before the relationship even gets off the ground?

~~~~~

Genre: Paranoraml Romance, Shifters
Featuring Tiger Shifter

Available in ebook and print

Claiming More
Tiger Nip, Book 2

TEZ Publishing

Sampson Hart has known Mary Jane Poppy for ten years. She's his sister's best friend, business partner, and has had a crush on Sam for years. When the mating pull hits him, he's ready to claim her as his own. Given their history, it should be simple. Right?

MJ has loved Sam since she was fifteen. But being a hybrid, she's been told all her life she won't have a mate. When Sam proclaims she belongs to him, she doesn't believe it; the mating pull isn't there, and Sam isn't meant to be hers.

Running back home to escape the love she feels for Sam, MJ agrees to become the companion of a man who lost his mate and has three young children to raise. It is the only way to set Sam free to find the one he is truly meant to be with.

Will Sam be Claiming More or will the one he desires the most find comfort in the arms of another?

~~~~~

Genre: Paranoraml Romance, Shifters
Featuring Tiger Shifter

Available in ebook and print

Dallas & Kacie: Tiger Bite
Tiger Nip, Book 2.5

TEZ Publishing

It's the holiday season and Kacie Cook is counting down the hours until its time to close up Sweet Confections. Not that she has any great plans for the week the bakery is closed. She won't be seeing her family—yet again, and all of her friends are too busy. All she has planned is a little rest and relaxation. That is until the last customer of the night walks in. Could he be the one to bring some holiday cheer and possibly change her life forever?

~~~~~

Genre: Paranoraml Romance, Shifters
Featuring Tiger Shifter

ABOUT THE AUTHOR

Brandy is a paranormal romance author who, on occasion, likes to dabble with contemporary. She's addicted to MDK shows and who-done-its. You'll almost never see her without some type of skull paraphernalia on and is always dreaming of more tattoos.

Brandy is a Navy brat, prior enlisted Army, current Army wife, and mom. She lives in Virginia with her husband of almost 20 years, their three kids and one dog.

Brandy is all over the web. Pick one or all to keep up with her.

Don't forget to sign up for the newsletter. There is a monthly giveaway and when the mood strikes other fun things like deep discounts in the shop.

www.brandywalker.net

facebook.com/BrandyWalkerfanpage

twitter.com/Brandy_W

OTHER BOOKS BY BRANDY WALKER

TEZ PUBLISHING

Tiger Nip

Craving More, Book 1

Claiming More, Book 2

Dallas & Kacie: Tiger Bite, Book 2.5

Finding More, Book 3 (future release)

Giving More, Book 4 (future release)

Seeing More, Book 5 (future release)

Freefall

Caught in the Moment, Book 1

Fly Guy Next Door, Book 2

Captured by Color, Book 3 (future release)

Revving Her Engine, Book 4 (future release)

Spinning Out of Control, Book 5 (future release

Mystic Zodiac

Thane | January | Angel

Parvati | February | God/Goddess

Gideon | March | Shifter

Lisa | April | Nymph (releasing Apr 2015)

Celeste | May | Fae (releasing May 2015)

Willow | June | Witch/Warlock (releasing Jun 2015)

Amber | July | Siren (releasing Jul 2015)

Adrian | August | Dragon (releasing Aug 2015)

Colby | September | Djinn (releasing Sep 2015)

Lucas | October | Vampire (releasing Oct 2015)

Mace | November | Spirit (releasing Nov 2015)

Falcon | December | Demon (releasing Dec 2015)

Keystone Predators

Under Her Spell (releasing Jun 2015)

Praetorian Guards

New series in the works

DECADENT PUBLISHING

ROAR LINE

Shifter U

Shifted Plans, Book 1

Changing Her Tune, Book 2 (future release)